Honestly!

Thank you Don

John Queen

ONE

Our Odyssey

D1607514

John C. Queen

Cover design by Linda Starkey

Interior design by Rosalie S. Krenger

ISBN: 9798850535612

CONTENTS

PROLOGUE

Us

And then it was here, four billion years ago, hanging in all the black darkness. Blue. A little blue dot, so small, insignificant, and yet somehow, someway, in just the right spot.

Circling a star, the blue turns, making day and night. All that we would become, everything that would live and die, circles the sun.

Come with me to this little blue dot, see the sun shining on the blue water, the waves crashing on the shore. Watch the sun patiently shining on the waves, waiting; it has so much time. Millions of eons, the earth turns, making a circle - billions upon billions of circles. Then, finally, something begins to happen in the water.

Look.

Stand with me and look down at the water. Do you see them?

Those are living cells. Out of nothing, something is alive. *Alive.*

The brave little blue dot turns some more, collides with others; massive explosions erupt from the surface, then there is land. Land, where we would walk and live. Can you feel the land under your feet?

Now listen and hear the ocean waves meet the land, crashing on the shore. Stand with me at the ocean's edge and listen. Can you hear?

Now kneel. Kneel with me; get down on your knees, bend your head low, as if in prayer. See the first cell divide. Then another, and another, and another, and another.

Eons pass. Now the little blue dot is covered with plants, trees, rivers, and mountains; it teems with life. Flying in the air, swimming in the water, creeping and crawling on the land.

• • •

On the land, a bipedal mammal walks and runs upright. A large hard skull, filled with soft tissue, sending, and receiving bits of electrical and chemical messages. On the end of both forearms is a hand, a thumb that complements four fingers.

On her back, an infant hangs on to life.

She kneels by the blue water, sees her reflection.

"Me?" she asks. She moves her head up and down, back and forth. "Yes, it is me." She looked up at the sky, "That does not end—how? Who am I? Why am I here? What are these feelings of joy, sadness, life, and death? Am I special; did something create me?" She looks back at the water and then to the sky again. Her mind spins with possibilities.

The infant on her back peeks over a shoulder; seeing its reflection in the water, it jerks its head to the other side. Then sees its reflection again and makes a sound. The mother moves the child to her breast. Milk flows. She sighs and strokes his head softly.

He is her second child. The first died when she turned her back, when the ones with teeth took it. She'd shed tears for the first time from a pain that was not a wound to her body. This pain was deep inside. The scar is still there, never to leave.

She strokes her son's head again, rocking him as he nurses. He finishes and she moves him to her back once more.

She cups her hand and gets a drink of water, sees a smooth rock by the water and picks it up. It fits her hand perfectly; she opens and closes her hand around the stone. Images of the ones with teeth flash in her mind. Perhaps... maybe a chance? She holds the stone tightly.

The rock becomes so much more.

Rock in hand, one of our mothers stands up, her son on her back, and walks away, joining others, multiplying, creating, and evolving until the little blue dot is covered with us.

• • •

Of all the living things that came out of the water, one mammal dips a feather in ink to write. He smooths papyrus with the palm of his hand and begins to write on a surface that is as flat as he believes his Earth to be. The reflection of his own face fills his eyes.

The feather moves on papyrus, black ink flowing.

"God created heaven and earth." (Genesis 1:1) "God created man in his own image." (1:27) "God blessed them and said to them, 'Be fruitful and multiply, and fill the earth and subdue it; rule over the fish of the sea and the birds of the air and every creature that crawls upon the earth.'" (Genesis 1:28.)

Across an ocean, the Hopi story of creation speaks of a spider woman who mixes her saliva with dirt, creating two beings. Her only instruction: to respect all creation.

In another culture of this world, the Egyptian god Atum weeps, and the tears bring human beings into existence. *Tears.*

We agree to disagree on how we got here in our own holy books, legends, and faiths. Each story changes, yet so much stays the same. We come from something, rise from somewhere.

The one indisputable fact is that we are here, all of us. Consuming towards oblivion. We have used the waters we emerged from and the air we breathe as our slit trench. The rock is now a missile, thrown thousands of miles.

We teeter on the edge of destruction. This is not a myth, legend, or statement of faith.

Now we cry, "God save us."

Listen.

What do you hear?

The silence is frightening.

— 1 —

Empty

God's silence is broken by a hungry mother's shout.

"Hurry Ahmad, they will not wait. The line is growing! Hurry!"

She motions him towards the flap covering the tent's entrance. The boy runs to the trench behind the tents, pulls down his ragged pants, and defecates into a ditch. Others squat with him. He stands, pulls up his pants, and wipes his hands on his shirt as he runs back to the tent.

Their sandals make tracks in the dry dust as they leave their tent, dusty sacks in hand; there is not a blade of grass in sight. Small hills to the east are dotted with stumps, the trees gone for firewood. The burned skeleton of a pickup truck lies on its side. A blackened tank sits on top of the hill. Two men with rope and knives chase a dog past the tank. The sun is obscured by the dust that coats the ugly brown sky.

A slight wind lifts the dust as it moves with the mother and son. The dog cries.

A young woman with a crying baby strapped to her back runs past them. An older man, his shoulders stooped, pants as he walks. He glances at them as they pass and mutters, "It will be all gone."

They walk with others who carry containers in their hands—buckets, boxes, or sacks. A throng of people moves to the trucks in the distance. As they near, hurriedly, men in uniforms holding guns force them into a line they willingly become.

Ahmad's mother runs her hand over his matted black hair. She sees the dirt on his scalp, looks at him with tired eyes. There are no tears on her cheeks, just sadness about her—the way she stands, her shoulders stooped, head bowed; there is no pride left.

I am the mother; I cannot feed my child. I see no possibilities. Her mind is a chorus of despair.

Her son leans towards her. They stand and wait, moving forward occasionally as voices in the line murmur, "Will there be any left?"

An hour passes. The mother and the boy reach the serving line. Tables are set up in front of three trucks emblazoned with the letters UNICEF. People in uniforms stand behind large buckets of lentils and rice, dumping scoops of food into waiting containers for those in line. Each scoop is the same size, regardless of the size of the container.

"Please, more," those with large containers plead desperately. The reply is always the same: a shake of the head, or silence.

An older woman turns back to the mother. "When I was a young mother, we had so much to eat we threw leftover food to the dogs. Now dogs are food. We stand in line, our hands in front of us. How did we get here?"

They reach the tables, get the allotted amount of rice and lentils, and return to their tent.

The mother gets out a pot, dumps water and their rations into it, and puts it on to the small fire.

She watches the water boil, stirring occasionally, saying nothing. The only sound is the boiling water.

Ahmad sits by her, waiting, holding his empty bowl silently.

She turns off the fire and ladles the soup into two bowls. They each take a bowl and eat. When there seems to be no more, the mother takes Ahmad's bowl and, after inspecting it, hands it back to him.

"Ahmad, all." She points at one grain of rice in the bowl.

He takes his thumb and index fingernails' black edges, gets the last grain of white rice, and puts it in his mouth.

The mother looks at the pot grimly. "It is empty, Ahmad. Empty." She lowers her head. The meal is finished.

Silence fills the tent. A gust of wind blows dust in and the mother shakes her head, looking at the brown dirt below her.

• • •

Green grass borders the sidewalk on Maple Street in White Plains, New York. A young man carrying a pizza box walks to the front door of a modest two-story white house and rings the doorbell.

A dog's high-pitched bark echoes behind the door before a huge man opens it, saying, "Great! We were hoping it was the pizza man! Ignore the poodle. It just barks." He hands the young man some money, "Thank you."

He closes the door and walks to his living room, where a plump girl sits on the couch, watching a cartoon on a large television.

"Jordan, supper is here."

"Good, I am so hungry," says Jordan, ruffling her straight, clean, freshly combed brown hair. "I feel so good after my shower. I sweat so much today."

The man sits down, sighing as his butt hits the couch. His belly droops over his belt. "Yeah, I did too. The heat today was almost unbearable. One hundred and seven degrees; a new record for New York!"

He opens the pizza box lid; there are two paper plates on the table. "Help yourself." He takes two slices, puts them on his plate, and leans back into the sofa. His clean, pale skin and white teeth stain slightly as he bites into the pizza. His fat neck shakes some as he eats and swallows.

Jordan's clean hands pick up a piece of pizza. She bites, chews, swallows, and then licks the sauce off her shiny fingernails.

They both eat silently as the cartoon plays on the television. The girl takes a piece of pepperoni off the pizza and hands it to the tiny white poodle sitting by her feet. The dog takes the pepperoni, chomps quickly, and swallows. Then it licks its lip and looks up for another.

"That's enough," her father says, "Corky will get sick, and you will have to clean it up." She nods.

They keep taking pizza out of the box. Hands to box to mouth, chewing, then swallowing.

They eat all but one piece of pizza.

"Had enough?" the man asks.

"Stuffed," she sighs.

The man gets up, groaning as he rises, the box in one hand, the other holding his can of soda. He walks out the apartment's back door to the garbage can outside, where he lifts the top and drops the pizza box.

The lid of the pizza box comes open as it hits the can, and the piece of pepperoni pizza hits the ground.

The man doesn't notice; he goes back into the apartment, groaning from exertion as he climbs the three steps into the back door.

· · ·

Sunrise.

A fat rat is exploring the area around the trash can. She puts her front paws on the side, stretching, her nose twitching and sniffing. The rat goes around to the side of the trash can. She sees the piece of pizza, grabs it, and runs.

She finds her way to the gutter, stops for one bite, and runs past pedestrians with the piece of pizza clamped in her teeth, hurrying home.

Soon she curls up, and ten young suck life from her; pepperoni and crust lay beside her. The rat closes her eyes as the young nurse. She is content.

· · ·

On the other side of the world, a dog carcass turns on a spicket over coals, and the aroma of cooking meat reaches Ahmad, who rolls in his bed. He puts his hands on his sunken stomach and cries out, "Mama, I am hungry!"

The mother holds back a sob.

Silence fills the tent.

— 2 —

Rattus Norvegicus

New York City, June 2030

The smog blocks the sunlight, buildings reach into the gray, their tops hidden. Morning traffic fills the street, smog slowing the movement of the cars whose tires and horns screech; an occasional curse word is screamed from an open car window. Pedestrians cram the sidewalk. Some wear face masks others have a transparent plastic hose running to a compact oxygen concentrator strapped to their belt or small backpack. They wipe their foreheads as the early morning temperature has already exceeded 80 degrees.

• • •

The crowd of pedestrians comes to a crosswalk, and all obediently stop. Men turn to look at an attractive blond in business attire, and the barest smile plays across her red-tinted lips.

Something stirs to the right of the crowd of pedestrians in the gutter, and they turn to look at it. She turns to see what the rest of the group is staring silently at and sees a rat carrying a slice of pepperoni pizza.

"Rat!" she screams.

Standing at the curb, close to the rat, is a thin man with hair so blonde that it's almost white, contrasting sharply against his cinnamon-colored skin.

He looks at the woman and says, matter-of-factly, "Homo sapiens discard food. Rattus norvegicus finds the food and eats it. Nine million Homo Sapiens in New York vs. thirty million Rattus Norvegicus." His intense concentration is on the rat. He looks at it as if he has never seen one before, occasionally taking pictures with a camera. "How much food is being thrown away to support thirty million of these mammals? Why are they throwing food away while so many Homo Sapiens go hungry?" His voice is soft, deep, filled with wonder and curiosity as he bends to look at the rat more closely. "How much?"

The man once again becomes lost in his study of the rat and moves gracefully, changing the weight from one side of his body to the other as he focuses the camera. The woman watches him squatting down on his haunches. She barely hears him mumble, "Is that pepperoni? I love pepperoni."

The light changes, and the pedestrians move on. The man stays, looking at the rat.

The rat stops running in the gutter, takes a bite out of the pizza, then sniffs the air as it stands on its rear legs. After a moment, it picks up its meal again and runs, disappearing down a storm drain.

Satisfied, the man walks to the corner kiosk for his usual coffee. He is looking at this camera as he walks, considering the pictures he took. He is so engrossed that he does not see the blonde woman from before standing in a shop's doorway on her phone.

She sees him and watches him walk by, moving with that same uncommon grace. His feet touched the pavement easily, softly. His shoes must never wear out, she thinks.

He walks up to the kiosk.

"Good morning, Sam," he says to the man inside.

Sam's friendly smile is real and inviting on his round, caramel-colored face. Short, balding, and with plump cheeks, he seems the kind of person that is pleasant to be around. Sam greets the photographer warmly.

"Good morning, Bob. Good to see you again. Usual coffee with four sugars?"

Bob smiles, "Yep, you got it. I'm always excited for your excellent coffee."

As Sam gets the coffee, he spots the camera. "What do you have there?"

Bob puts his camera in his shoulder bag and explains, "There was a Rattus Norvegicus by the curb this morning as I came out of the apartment. Nothing new, but there was a woman who was fearful of it. I explained it was simply eating - it had a piece of pizza. Pepperoni, I think. I got some pictures; I believe its mammary glands are enlarged."

Sam blinks. "Rattus norvegicus means, rat I assume?"

"You are correct. The 'Rattus' part does give it away."

Ignoring the jab, Sam asks, "Enlarged, mammary glands? What do you mean? Is that rat infected with something?"

"No," says Bob without any judgment, "she is not infected. Enlarged mammary glands would mean she is nursing her young. On the human female, I have heard men calling them boobs, knockers, or tits."

Just as the word "tits" comes out of his mouth, the blonde from before steps up to the counter. She looks at Bob with disgust, shaking her head.

Sam sets the coffee down on the counter and looks at Bob. "Four dollars. Thanks for the nature lesson."

Bob hands over the money. "You're welcome. The English language can be confusing. All those names for one body part!" With that final comment, he walks away.

Sam looks at the woman. "What can I get for you today?"

She smiles, "Definitely coffee! Plain and simple, please." As Sam begins her order, she asks, "Who is that guy? He gave me a quick lesson on the population levels of rats and humans. Apparently, the rats are winning. I watched him take a picture of a rat carrying a piece of pizza and then ask the rat if the pizza was pepperoni. Thankfully, the rats haven't mastered speech yet, and it didn't answer."

Sam laughs. "No need to worry about Bob. A harmless guy knows a lot about everything. He's from somewhere in Europe, I think? Says he's a writer and photographer. Free-lance. You never know what he is going to say. I will say he's a little different. Spectrum stuff, maybe?" He shrugs. "What can I put in the coffee for you?"

"Oh, four sugars, please," the woman replies. "I will admit that it was a unique experience, seeing a guy talk to a rat. He has an interesting accent that I couldn't place. Africa, maybe?" Sam shakes his head—he doesn't know, either—and she returns the shrug. "Oh well. New York, my first day; it shouldn't surprise me. What do I owe you for the coffee?"

"What's your name, miss?"

"Grace. Just moved in a couple of days ago."

"And where are you off to on your first day out?"

"I'm going to check out summer school for my son. He's coming tomorrow, so I hope it's as good as the reviews say."

Sam smiles. "Coffee on me today, then. If you like it, come back. Good luck, Grace. I hope it goes well for you and your son."

The woman smiles in surprise. "Thank you! What's your name?"

"Sam. Sam Gonzales."

"Been here long, Sam?"

"Fifteen years. I got out of Columbia and brought my family here while you still could. Thankful that my children are not in that part of the world."

"Thanks, Sam," she says with a smile, tipping the coffee cup toward him.

Sam waves as she turns and walks towards the subway entrance, coffee in hand. She sees Bob standing at the curb, talking on his phone, but ignores him and heads down to the subway below.

Grace is almost down the stairs to board the Metro, paying more attention to not tripping than who is around her, when a gaunt, emaciated youth with a baseball cap pulled down low over his forehead makes his move. He sprints up the stairs, grabs the purse strap on Grace's shoulder, and pulls.

Grace loses her balance and falls back, but the wall catches her just in time. The coffee flies in the air.

"My purse!" She shouts, "Stop him!"

Bob, having apparently heard this, turns just in time to see the youth running with the purse, and Grace against the wall. The kid is only concentrating on one thing: speed. As he reaches Bob, Grace watches Bob tilts his head forward just a bit, look directly at the kid, and say something she cannot hear.

The kid's right leg crosses in front of the left, and he trips, falling on the sidewalk. The purse slides a few feet in front of him; Bob steps over and picks it up.

"My ankle!" the youth moans, glaring up at Bob. "Goddamn you, how did you trip me?"

Bob doesn't answer but makes no move to further apprehend him, so the youth stands up and hobbles away as quickly as he can, not keen on any more trouble.

"What happened?" Grace says, running over.

Bob looks at her and says simply, "He tripped." He hands Grace her purse.

"Well," Grace says, rattled, "I'm glad you were here to help. Did you trip him?" She hadn't seen Bob move to do so.

"No, I just told him to stop," Bob says, then asks, "Are you injured?"

"No, just flustered. Why didn't the kid just ask me for money? My God, how desperate do you have to be to steal a purse in broad daylight? I would have given him money if he had asked!" She stops to take a breath and collect herself, then starts again. "You're the guy from Sam's, right? The rat population expert?"

"Yes, I am. I apologize for my locker talk," he says quietly. "Beauty is on the inside."

He is leaning slightly towards her, eyes totally focused on her. Bob seems oblivious to all around him: the noise, the people, the foul air. He stands as a stone and sees only her, and the rest of the world does not exist.

Grace sees his green eyes looking only at her eyes and not looking at the plunging v-neck blouse. They don't stray to her red lips; they focus just on her eyes. Different, she thinks. Her confident stance shrinks, and she looks away at nothing, only to glance back and see only his eyes. This time, there is no slight smile on her lips. She moves one hand to her chest above the blouse.

Quietly, she says, "Thanks for the help with the purse. Have a good day." Grace continues down the subway steps and is gone.

Bob's phone rings. He answers, still looking after Grace.

"Yes," he says to the voice at the end of the line, "you can pick me up at Sam's. I can be there in five minutes. Do you want a cup of coffee?"

Bob walks back towards Sam's, watching the morning commuters walk towards the train station. Most look at their phones as they shuffle along, breathing units making a *puff, puff* sound. He steps into the traffic, staying to the right as they stream by him, silent. He watches their faces and looks at their eyes. They could have been machines stepping forward into the smog.

When he arrives, Sam greets him just as warmly as before. "Hey, back for a refill?"

"Catching a cab, need one for the driver. Four sugars, please."

"You got it. One coffee, coming up," Sam says as he starts to work. "Wow, it's hot already. The air smells so bad with the exhaust fumes, and there's been no breeze for days. The entire city is trapped in the same air. When is this going to change for the better? I can't talk to customers wearing a breathing unit."

Sam sets the coffee on the counter. No longer smiling, he looks at Bob, wiping the sweat off his brow. "I'd bet you didn't know earlier that the woman was standing behind you when you talked about tits."

"I would not have used the slang words for the body part if I had known," Bob says wryly, "My assumption at the time was that only males were present. The correct scientific description is mammary glands." He pauses, then says, "I watched her go down to the subway. She is what most males describe as 'hot.' She does have exterior beauty." He shrugs. "Exterior beauty decreases. The interior beauty can grow. Beauty, such an interesting word."

Sam chuckles at this assessment. "You know, you're right. The outside fools most men. My wife is short, 'too heavy' if you know what I mean. Her...well, to be correct, her 'mammary glands' are starting to sag. Today though, I see her interior. My wife is beautiful," Sam's smile returns once more.

"Beautiful. Used here primarily to describe the exterior of things, and we have used it for the interior, the inside of your wife and the woman from before. Looking inside, ignoring the outside." Bob stops, looks around, sees no one, and continues. "Did I upset your customer?"

"I would say she found you...different. I mean, you *were* taking pictures of a rat and its mammary glands. She said it was ok; it's New York City. Anything can happen here. So, no, you didn't upset her," Sam says.

"I think I may have made her rethink my position here in this place. A young male, barely out of puberty, attempted to steal her carrying device."

"Is she ok? Did the guy escape? Damn crooks," Sam says.

"Well, he asked God to damn me, then tripped and limped away. Complained about his ankle. Asking a deity to damn me seemed odd," Bob says, shaking his head some, looking at Sam for explanation.

"You didn't try to stop him?" Sam's lips are tight, the smile gone.

"No. I had recovered the private property of the woman that was buying coffee here earlier. My first concern was her. Sam, do you know her name?"

"Grace. She said her first name is Grace. She's new here, looking for a school for her son today, apparently."

"The name matches her. She has grace internally too," Bob smiles to himself, thinking of her.

"What do you mean?"

Bob says, in a softer voice, "She was puzzled the youth did not just ask her for money. She told me she would give it to him. Think about it. One person wanted to give something away, and the other did not ask. Neither is mute nor deaf; both speak the same language. How strange."

Sam shrugs his shoulders and looks at Bob.

"Something you wanted to ask me, Sam? Do you have an inquiry? Seeking data? My cab will be here soon," Bob questions his friend.

Sam just shakes his head and smiles another toothy grin. "No. I'm glad you helped the lady with the purse."

Bob walks away to the corner to wait for his cab.

A woman walks by, holding a small girl by the hand, impatiently urging her to hurry. "Simone, we will miss our train." The girl is holding a bag of bite-size crackers in her other hand, unknowingly sprinkling some on the pavement.

Pigeons aggressively harvest the bounty, then fly away. A man shouts as the pigeons fly above him, "God damn things!" He tries to wipe the pigeon poop from his shoulder with a white handkerchief.

The pigeons fly over Bob. He turns to watch their curve through the sky and points his finger, eyes full of wonder, voice loud and full of emotion as he talks to the birds.

"Feathers, on two paired forelimbs. Creating lift! Airfoil! You can fly, how beautiful. You fly! You fly! Amazing!" Bob shouts as he watches the birds continue to fly away.

The commuters look at him, shaking their heads in disbelief, like he is crazy in their eyes, but Bob doesn't notice. His face glows with excitement.

— 3 —

Looking for a Miracle

Grace steps over the spilled coffee, holding her purse tight. The damp air moves up the stairs to the street above, smelling of machinery and people. Her nose twitches just a bit in the foul air. The people moving down the stairs are solemn, quiet, jockeying for position.

She successfully navigates the stairs and studies the subway map. A man leans against the wall beside it, a dirty black stocking cap riding atop his ears. He is unshaven, shoulders slumped, with a duffel bag at his feet. Grace tries to avoid him, but she cannot escape his sunken eyes.

"Have any help for me?" he asks. His voice deep bass, breaking with emotion, speaking slowly, like time did not matter.

Grace reaches into her purse. "I have money. Here you go. What's your name?"

"Billy." He takes the money and reaches into his pocket, pulling out a Bible. He holds it up and reads, "You make a life by what you give. Mathew 6:38." He looks up. "Thank you for your generosity. May the Lord bless you, keep you, and give you peace."

His voice grows softer at the end of each phrase; he has it memorized, which is obvious; it is impossible not to hear it, even though it's quiet.

"Thank you, Billy," Grace replies, touched by his profound words and, wanting to offer something, adds, "Do you like coffee?"

"Yes, I do. What's your name, Miss?"

"Grace," she says.

"Grace, meaning 'God's favor.'"

"Yes, my mother named me." She smiles and looks around. "Billy, are you here every morning?"

"Yes, this is my spot. I have a grocery cart, too, but I have it hidden from the thieves. They are about." He glances around as if searching for something in the crowd.

"Good for you, Billy. You're right; they're about. I'll see you again. Have a good day."

"Grace, Grace, I will be here. Thank you again." He bows his head toward her, quietly saying, "God's favor," before turning on his heel and disappearing into the crowd.

Grace makes her way to the boarding platform, pushing through the people standing shoulder to shoulder, waiting. Some wipe sweat from their foreheads. She can hear a portable oxygenator unit's sound of rhythmic puffing. She looks across the tracks to the other side, covered with plastic soda bottles, sandwich wrappers, and newspapers strewn carelessly about. Moving among the litter is a rat.

"Mommy, look! It's a big, big mouse!" a little girl cries out.

The mother replies, "That is a rat. It's probably looking for something to eat over there."

Grace smiles, "Yes. The odds are extremely high that it will find something."

The little girl whines, "Mommy, I'm hungry."

The mom sighs. "You should have eaten all of your cereal at breakfast—such a waste." Grace nods silently in agreement. In her mind, she sees the rat running with the pizza.

The train pulls up and stops. The doors open, and Grace and her companions enter, faces contorting as they inhale creosote, steel dust, and body odor. She finds a seat next to the window. The mother and child stop beside her. The mother says, "Do you mind?" She smiles, as does the little girl, maybe 7 years old.

Grace smiles in return, "Absolutely. I would love to have company."

"Thanks. In New York; you never know if someone wants anyone sitting by them. The heat makes them more irritable; I think. There are so many people here."

"Yes," Grace agrees, "I was told this morning there were approximately nine million people versus thirty million rats. It's no small wonder your daughter saw one."

The mother blinks in shock. "Thirty million! It sounds like you had an interesting morning."

Grace chuckles. "Do you want to hear it? I can also tell you about being robbed and saved!"

The train leaves the station, and Grace recounts her strange commute from the rat to the man with the camera and the excellent coffee. Her mind keeps wandering back to him, and she finishes her story by saying, "He...well, he looked at me in a way I've never experienced before."

"What do you mean?"

"He looked into me. It was weird, nothing I've ever experienced before," Grace says.

"What an interesting man being calm in all of this," the mother agrees. "Temperature records being broken every day, oxygen level at 19%, the air smells, smog...well, you know. Did you get his name?"

"No, I didn't. I'm Grace, by the way. Grace De Falco. It's my first day on the Metro and second day in New York."

"I'm Erin Hood, and this is my daughter Simone." Simone waves.

"So, Erin, how do you decide if you need a mask or an oxygen concentrator? It appears about half of the people here have one."

"Yes, half of us look like we are going to a Halloween party. I've been in denial despite seeing this coming for a long time. I just didn't want to admit what was happening. The lithium-powered units, the good small ones, are three grand. The truth, of course, is that the three grand won't fix the problem, but Simone has asthma. We're going to her pulmonologist; he'll check her breathing with and without the unit. I'm sure she'll come home with one."

"What do you mean, you saw this coming?"

"I work for the National Oceanic and Atmosphere Administration," Erin says, "I've documented phyto-plankton concentrations and ocean temperatures for the last 10 years."

Grace looks at her seriously. Waits for her to go on.

"I'll just say one is going up while the other is going down."

"Mommy says we used the oceans for a trash can," Simone butts in.

"What can be done?" Grace asks.

"We're working on some devices to clean the oceans. The problem is powering them with nonpolluting energy. We just need a clean source."

"White Plains. Next stop," the announcement blares in the train car. "White plains. Next stop."

The train slows. "This is my stop," Grace says as she stands up, "Please keep working on everyone's prob-lem. Have a wonderful day. Simone, I hope you get some-thing to eat."

Erin smiles at her. "That man, so interesting. Calm in all this. What did you learn this morning?"

"Lose the purse. Wear slacks with pockets!" Grace shouts.

"Or do this." Erin lifts her blouse just above her waist, revealing a holster, just below her naval, the pink handle of a gun visible. She lowers her blouse and looks at Grace. "Hunger, desperation, no hope. People will try anything. You must be ready for anything. So thankful the man was able to help you. Hope you get to see him again."

"One in nine million? I doubt it."

Grace exits the train and starts her way up the stairs, only to stop as an elderly man in front of her pauses to catch his breath.

"Sorry." The word comes out hoarsely, in the exhale of a breath; the old man looks at her, shoulders slumped forward, a hand on the rail, panting. "I can't afford a breathing unit," he says.

She nods, moves around him, and walks up to the sidewalk.

Her phone vibrates; she pulls it out of her purse. The screen says, "John De Falco."

She answers. "Good morning, John." Pause. "Yes, I got settled in simply fine. Jack has a nice room. I'm going to the school to check it out and then on to my first day at Parabola Systems."

She listens again. "Yes, sure you can join the interview. I'm sure you'll have questions."

Grace moves out of the pedestrian traffic listening on her phone. "Okay, I'll call you at 9. Thank you again for agreeing to let me have Jack for the summer. I am so excited to see him." She listens some more. "Wow, well he is 11. Puberty. I will be ready. I will try. Talk to you at 9."

She puts her phone away, rubs one finger over the place where the ring used to be, and walks on.

She reaches a crosswalk and stops. Across the street, she sees a red sign above a storefront that reads, "Breathe 21% Oxygen! Concentrator Units, rent or buy."

The light changes: the crowd of pedestrians moves through the smog silently. Grace moves with them. She takes a deep breath to get as much oxygen as possible. Occasionally, she rubs her face, feeling like the air has deposited something on it, looking at her hand to find nothing.

She passes more people on the sidewalk, begging as she walks to the school. Her lips mouthing, "Sorry." Finally, she quits looking at them.

Ten minutes later, she reaches the school. A sign above the entrance with colorful lettering reads: "Endless Possibilities." Caricatures of children play below the lettering. Grace walks up to the entry door and sees a man behind a window in the foyer. He smiles at her.

At the top of the glass, she sees in large print, 'PHOTO ID REQUIRED.'

The man's voice booms out a greeting. "Good morning! How may I help you?"

"My name's Grace De Falco. I'm here to meet with Ms. Alana. My son Jack may attend summer school here?"

He answers, "Good morning, Miss De Falco. Can you put your driver's license in the drawer? You are on the list, so I just need to verify." Grace puts her driver's license in the drawer, eyeing the thick glass between her and the man. He puts the driver's license in a scanner. "This will take a minute or so."

After a minute, the door clicks and swings open. The man is at least six feet tall and looks about 300 pounds. Grace's eyes open wide at this massive cylinder of a man. There is no stomach hanging over the belt. She takes in his light brown hair, smooth face, warm smile, and eyes that twinkle, noticing a pistol holster strapped to his belt.

"I'm Herschel, the school's head of security. I'll walk you back. Here is your driver's license," he says, handing her the card. "I buzzed Ms. Alana so she knows we're coming. Are you comfortable breathing? We have an excellent air filtering system."

Grace takes a deep breath. "Oh, yes! I can tell the difference. The subway was, well, challenging to say the least." She keeps glancing at the gun.

Herschel sees her looking at it. "Yes, I am armed. That is bulletproof glass you were looking at, and our facial recognition system is the best we can buy. We also have bulletproof doors in our classrooms. There are other devices that are offensive in nature. Those are confidential. I can assure you your child will be safe here. My mission is to protect these children," his voice is still friendly but firm.

As they walk down the wide hall, Herschel asks, "Where do you work, Grace?"

"Parabola Systems. I can walk here, so it would be convenient. I hope this works."

Herschel chuckles. "We'll love having your son here! You won't believe what we're doing here. I love this job."

"You love your job?"

"I do. I get to watch parents come and interact with their children before they leave and entrust them to our capable hands. I see children grow and change here; it gives me hope."

"I'm still a bit concerned," Grace says nervously.

"What's your son's name?" Herschel asks.

"Jack. His name is Jack De Falco," Grace answers.

"Jack!" Herschel replies with a reassuring smile. "I like that name! I look forward to meeting him."

A woman walks toward them. "Good morning, Ms. De Falco. Thank you for being a little early. And thank you, Herschel, for bringing her back."

Herschel nods to Grace. "It was so nice to meet you, Grace." He turns and walks back to his station.

Ms. Alana leads Grace into the classroom. The chairs are arranged in a circle toward the center, and educational posters cover the walls. Ms. Alana motions for Grace to sit with her.

Grace's knee bounces a bit. She puts a calming hand on it.

After making some plain small talk, Ms. Alana says with a smile, "Please tell me about Jack."

"Before we start, let me call my husb— Jack's father. He wanted to listen in." Ms. Alana nods her head.

"John, good morning again. You are on speaker, I am with "Ms. Alana.""

"Good morning Mr. De Falco. Good to have you with us."

"Good morning Ms., Alana. I have read a few things about the school. Sounds like you are doing amazing things with children."

"Yes, we are. Amazing staff, support from the parents. We believe we prepare these children in a unique way. Just butt in if you have a question. Grace was just getting ready to tell me about Jack, Grace please continue."

Grace begins slowly, "Our Jack is brilliant. He remembers most of what he reads and is completely honest. However, I should let you know that he's on the spectrum, so he exhibits some…different behaviors; he talks loudly, flaps his hands, misses many social clues, and is completely honest - almost to a fault."

"Most of our students have something that makes them stand out. We have students with many different traits and gifts. Part of what we do here is to get the student to recognize the gifts. I'm sure Jack will fit in well."

Grace looks at Ms. Alana. She has a sense of calmness about her, as though nothing could rattle her.

"Alana, I'm not sure you understand. Jack can be frustrating at times."

"I'm sure you are correct. How old is Jack?"

"Eleven. John jump in if you want."

"Yeah, thank you Grace. Yes, completely honest, saying things that are out of the norm, talking about his physical body as it changes. 'Why armpit hair?' was his latest question to me. While we were standing in a check out line at the grocery store. Not the best place to ask that question."

Ms. Alana smiles. "Puberty. A perfect time for him to be in a school like this."

"Please explain. Why would this school be different from any other?" John asks.

"We enable conversations between the children," Alana says without hesitation. "Many of our children are on the spectrum. They are all gifted in some way, yet they tend to have traits that can make developing friendships difficult, so developing friendships is a big part of our mission."

"Can you give me an example of enabling conversations?" Grace asks.

Alana obliges readily. "The first day Jack is here, he'll be with a group of children in a session we call 'Relax'. They introduce themselves to each other and just visit socially. I help to enable these conversations via modeling and prompting. It's my favorite day."

"I'm not sure he can do this," Grace says, "So many new people and places, and the move...This might frighten him." She stops to think about the whole situation before correcting herself, "No, it *will* frighten him."

"Yes, I agree, it will." John says.

"We all know life can be frightening," Alana soothes, "One of our main goals here is dealing with that fear. When Jack leaves here, he'll have the tools he needs to deal with what frightens him."

"How do you accomplish that?" Grace asks.

"By being around others on the spectrum, each child learns to realize others have their traits and ways of learning, too. We encourage these children to talk about who they are. Kids should not beat themselves up because their DNA coding is different; we all have things about ourselves we have been told we should like to change."

"Yes, I fall into that group," Grace jumps in.

"Exactly. Helping the children learn who they are and accept that is giving them a gift." Ms. Alana says. She stops, gathers her thoughts, and holds her hands together before continuing.

"Grace and John, a question. When you left your primary education, before you entered higher education, did you know your strengths and weaknesses? Could you answer the question, "Who am I?""

"No. Absolutely not," Grace's answer is direct, firm no.

"Nor I," John echoes.

"Neither did I. I was raised in a very conservative family, one way of looking at the world, yet there are many ways of seeing. I excluded so many people from my life at a younger age, and I regret that. We want these children to learn to accept each other."

"Jack knows all his quirks, differences, and he can name them. Eye contact, listening," Grace sighs.

Alana beams, smiles, "That's good! Is he comfortable with those quirks?"

"Not all of them, no."

Alana nods. "Some of Jack's traits are gifts. We'll help Jack recognize that and use them. Our job is to send these children into the world knowing who they are—their strengths, their weaknesses. With the way the world is now, we need these children."

"Okay," Grace says, leaning more into the conversation, "Tell me about your curriculum."

"Of course. We have teachers that are gifted in every subject. They're amazing; the teachers are, of course, the most important part of our school. They have experience with kids on the spectrum; most of our teachers have a child or grandchild on the spectrum. Excuse me, it sounds like preaching, but our teachers are here because they are dedicated to helping these kids."

Grace makes a mental note of this, then adds, "Jack has big questions about social issues and religion, so he asks many questions that are...way beyond the norm."

"We do a swift course on the major religions of the world and what they have in common," Alana says.

"Why do you include a course on the world's major religions?" John asks, his voice a bit tense.

"We don't endorse any religion, of course; we want our students to have some knowledge of the world's religions. We want them to listen to everyone, regardless of faith, without judging. We need everyone to solve the world's problems. We have had some parents who did not enroll their children because of our position on religion. That, of course, is their decision."

"Ms. Alana, I am Catholic, Jesus Christ is my lord and savior. What would you say about my faith?"

"Mr. Jeff teaches the religion class. He presents the facts of what Catholics believe. There are no opinions expressed."

"How do I know that?" John asks.

"Log in and watch the class. All our classes can be watched. We encourage it. Please, it helps us. You must agree to our rules, though: Critiques or compliments must be one on one, and no sharing of the video or social networking."

"I would be thrilled to watch Jack in class! And I like your rules." John says.

"Jack asks me why there are hungry people in the world. What kind of God would let a child starve when another throws food away. How would your instructors manage that one?" Grace says, frowning.

"Grace so many people in the world wait in line with an empty bowl," Alana replies, "saying 'feed me.' I've heard this question before, so this is Mr. Jeff's answer to these children: 'You are concerned and know that people are starving. That is good. First, figure out what world organizations are providing food and money to them. Then, raise money for that cause. I'll help you with the research.' Then Mr. Jeff might ask, 'Does anyone else want to work with Jack on this?'"

Alana's face gets more serious. "At the same time, we've heard questions that have no answers —death, sickness, suffering. You know. The list is long. We know if we encourage any questions, it will help the child deal with life's suffering."

Pleased with her answer, Grace asks, "Where do you get the money for all this? You have all this staff, security, the building. The tuition won't cover what you're doing."

"People talk about us. Donors appear, people who value what we are doing," says Alana. "Think of it; your son, Jack, who is highly intelligent. He could fill a need in the world. Our world needs that help; it needs to change."

Grace considers this woman carefully. "You talk like these children can do anything."

"Yes, yes, I do. We cannot wait for a miracle."

"We do need a miracle." John joins in.

They look at each other, silent. Grace is serious, Alana smiling.

"Okay," Grace says, "What do you think John? It sounds like this place could help Jack."

"Yes, it does. I am all in. Cannot wait to watch him in class. I need to sign off now. Have a good day."

They go to the desk, where Ms. Alana gives her a folder. "Just take this home with you, read at your convenience, and bring it back on Jack's first day."

Grace takes the folder. "Thank you."

"I'm excited to meet Jack."

With that parting, Grace walks down the hall to the front door, where Herschel still stands.

Grace smiles at him. "Is she real, this Ms. Alana?"

Herschel grins. "Some people are meant to be teachers. She is one of them. Jack will love it here, and you'll see why we all love working here."

"She talks about Jack and the children that come to this school as if they can do anything. As if they can help the world, even change it!"

Herschel stops smiling and adds, "I believe this."

Grace looks at him, "Wow. You're serious."

Herschel smiles again as he opens the door for her. "I'll watch for Jack De Falco. He will love it here!" Herschel assures her again as she walks away.

Grace sees another man approaching the school, with a boy walking beside him. The boy's eyes are on the ground as he viciously, continuously scratches his left arm.

The man talks to the boy in a very calm voice. "Here, Michael, try this instead." He hands the boy a small fidget toy, which he eagerly takes and begins to move rapidly between his hands. The man continues, "It's going to be fine. I've met this teacher. Once you meet her, you'll be just fine."

The boy's voice is nasal, whining. "My lungs are bothering me. I cannot breathe. When are we getting our units?"

"We'll be inside in just a minute. The air at the school is filtered so it'll be better inside. I'm a little short on money right now, so that'll have to do."

Grace walks on, taking deep breaths, her face solemn. She pulls out her phone, dials John again.

"What time do you think you'll arrive?" She listens, "Okay. I'll look for you around 4 p.m. You have the address, 9808 Mill, right? Okay, see you then."

— 4 —

In a Nanosecond

The pigeons are specks in the sky. Bob's head leans back, staring, watching them. A beeping horn interrupts him and a white Toyota pulls up to the curb. Bob slides into the back seat.

"Greetings, Don. Here is Sam's delicious coffee," Bob says, handing the coffee to the driver.

"Sam's coffee. I'm happy to accept!" He turns and takes the cup. He takes a sip. "Ahh, the sugar too. It's exactly right."

His face is excited as he utters the word sugar. "More cash in the envelope on the seat. Try not to give away so much. New phone. Same number, just new tools, and new protections. Instructions are to go by that decoy office and see if we've gathered any data from the listening devices."

"I will see if there are devices to scan. The data could reveal the purpose of the location." Bob leans forward, picking up the sealed envelope. "How are the rest?"

"Excellent. No difficulties. And you?" Don replied, not taking his eyes off the road.

Bob shakes his head. "It is puzzling to observe desperation. There is an abundance, yet there is a lack. I stopped a youth this morning who tried to take a woman's property. He might have weighed a hundred pounds at the most." He pauses. "Hunger."

"How'd you stop him?" Don asks, tension in his voice.

"Oh, he tripped. So easy to do when someone is starving and afraid. The woman was grateful. I sensed kindness in her," Bob said.

"Kindness?" Don asked.

"She would have given the youth money if he had asked. Strange. One has money to give, another does not ask."

As the cab pulls up the curb, the two men look directly at each other. Don's eyes are a dark blue, almost black. His skin tone is the same cinnamon as Bob's; his hair is the same white-blond under an NYC ball cap. There is a slight nod of unspoken agreement from both, and Bob opens the door and exits the cab silently.

He walks two blocks, approaching a building that says Bradford Real Estate Holdings in bold letters on the front. A man in a dark business suit walks into the building.

Bob walks down the street and turns the corner into an alley. He walks until he sees a sign above a door that also says Bradford Real Estate Holdings and a green dumpster beside it. He opens the lid, takes his phone out, and moves it above discarded paper coffee cups. The screen lights up, with the outline of a circle on the screen. The ring fills with dots until it is solid. In minutes, the phone goes dark, and Bob puts it back in his pocket while he closes the lid.

Just at that moment, the back door to the building opens, and the man who had walked into the front door stands there, his suit jacket unbuttoned and black leather gun holster on display. His dark eyes staring, a nose bulbous, black hair cut short, a stocky build. He leans forward as he shouts.

"Hey, asshole!" the man shouts, "There's nothing in there but paper cups and fast food containers. There's nothing for you to eat. Move on!" He slams the door shut.

Bob says nothing as he walks away.

He is stopped by a voice a few feet from him.

"Fear not, I am with you." A stocking cap rises above several trash cans; it's followed by a bearded face. "The man with the gun is like a breath; his days, a passing shadow. My God protects me," the voice is loud in the alley. The words 'protects me' ring with conviction.

"Neither that book nor a god will stop a bullet," Bob reaches into his pocket, pulls out a bill, handing it to the bearded man.

"I have been blessed twice today – the woman who God Favors and now you. Your days will not be a passing shadow," the man bows his head before shoving the money into his pocket.

"You are welcome. What name do you go by?" Bob asks.

"Billy, meaning, determined protector. What name do you go by?"

"Bob."

"Meaning bright, radiant," Billy says.

"Billy, stay away from that man, he is in darkness."

"I know all there is to know about darkness. I am not afraid," Billy says.

Bob studies this man's face, his eyes, then says, "Goodbye, determined protector."

"What was revealed to you in the trash?"

Bob pauses, but says nothing, realizing Billy had been watching him. He walks away, gets to the corner out of sight of the office, and dials a number.

"Yes, it worked. I will be in the area on Water Street."

Bob puts his phone in his pocket and starts walking. His gait is smooth, gliding along the streets of New York, passing the street vendors and cabs picking up rides. An occasional homeless person sits on the sidewalk, up against a building, holding a cup or sign, all saying the same thing.

Bob stops at each one, eagerly handing them a one-hundred-dollar bill. His expression does not change as he hears, "God bless you."

He turns the corner and starts down Water Street. He gets out his camera, pulls out a telescopic lens, and attaches it. People glance at him, but few pay attention. Most are dressed in expensive clothes, but all have breathing units. Bob sees bulges under clothing, recognizing that many are carrying firearms. They file past the never-ending outstretched hands of the homeless as if they are invisible.

Of all the people on the sidewalk, Bob feels it first. A small wisp of air moves across his face. A breeze.

He stops, observing the smog move slowly.

A breeze that started somewhere in the Atlantic Ocean, moving west, over Long Island, Long Beach, Brooklyn, up the Hudson River. The sky is getting lighter as the smog starts to clear. The pedestrians walk brisker, for some reason, most unaware that something had changed around them. Bob raises his right hand, his palm facing the breeze and he says, "ah, wind, wind, wind." Some of the pedestrian's glance at him when they hear the word, then turn away.

Bob watches the sky intently, then turns his camera up, following something only he can see. His face is excited as he swings the camera up rapidly, twisted into a grin of excitement as he takes pictures. He brings the camera down and thumbs through the images. Nods his head, pleased with the results. He takes the telescopic lens off the camera and places it in the bag.

His phone rings.

"Yes, pick me up at the Peregrine Falcon site," he replies and hangs up, quickly looking back up to the sky. He continues to watch the pigeons until he hears a horn honk and looks to see the white cab with Don behind the wheel. He steps over to the curb and opens the door and gets in the car.

"I got great pictures today of a falcon getting a pigeon—at least two hundred miles per hour in the dive. There are amazing creatures here! People never look up unless it is snowing or raining." He stops talking for a few seconds, then shaking his head slightly. "They would never see it coming. They are so unaware of what is around them," Bob says quietly.

"Bob, focus on our mission. Remember our mission," Don says, impatience in his voice.

"This could all be gone in a nanosecond. We know that. I want to record it," Bob replies calmly.

"I know. I am concerned about the mission. How did it go?" With that, Don hands Bob his phone. "Download. Let us see if we have anything to work with. Any problems?"

Bob takes the two phones and puts them tightly together. "I had my phone down in the trash container, but this sharp dressed guy stepped out and threatened me. A dark suit in this heat? Why? And that way, he displayed his shoulder holster with a gun in it. Do they think their guns will save them? What is wrong with them? The oxygen levels are dropping, and they carry guns! They are infantile!" Bob shakes his head.

"Did he say anything to you?" Don looks in the mirror back at Bob.

"Yes, he said there was nothing in there to eat. He assumed I was homeless, looking for food. He addressed me as an asshole. Asshole? Why, was it because I was looking in a waste receptacle? What reply would I give to that word? Despite the name-calling, I remained silent. The data from the cups had been recorded." He finishes the data transfer and hands Don his phone back. "Is the data intact? Did the recording devices work?"

"Yes, there is a lot here. I am sending it on. Should tell us what they are doing here. Their scanners did not detect the recording strands in the cups." Don nods his head and pushes buttons on his phone. "We should know in a few minutes what we have found."

"Have you received any data from our team in Washington?" Bob asks.

Don shakes his head, "No, the collection of data should be happening now or very soon. If successful, it could tell us what the payloads on the new warheads are. One of our team members has devices in the White House."

"How?"

"The President likes roses. The devices are in the roses in the bedroom. The president's wife likes them. She is his confidant."

"We may need other places to get data. They obviously make war plans at the Pentagon complex. I see on the maps of the area there is even a shopping mall next to it. A huge military cemetery is close, Arlington. A war planning complex, cemetery, and a shopping mall. Killing, burial, and shopping, all in one location," Bob says, a look of puzzlement on his face.

Don's phone rings. He answers and listens intently. "Are you sure?" There is a long silence. "You have confirmed this?" Silence. Another long pause, and he ends the call. His face is ashen, strained.

"Interesting. The conversation is in Arabic. We're not the only ones trying to find out if the Ohio class submarines have changed their warheads."

"Have they changed the warheads?" Bob asks with a strain in his voice.

"All of the Ohio Submarines will be armed with a new type of warhead. That is over 2,600 warheads they will change in their fleet of submarines. Why? What are they? Why would they change them all? All of them?" Don runs his hand through his hair, his voice soft, a whisper.

"What could this be? A new, what, bigger, more powerful bomb? Why? They have 2,600," Bob's voice is low, a strain in it, incredulous.

"This will be done at Kings Bay submarine base. The Americans could do it there undetected in their gigantic dry dock. The President, of course, would know. Will he confide this with his spouse? Do they share terrible secrets?" Bob asks.

"We have team members spread along the Atlantic coast at different military installations. I am going to move some of them to Kings Bay," Don says.

"Kings Bay submarine base and the President of the United States bedroom. Where else can we look?"

"There are people in Washington D.C. besides the president who know what is on these new warheads. Bob, go to Washington, see if there is someone else besides the President that we could get data from. We must get the information first for the plan to work," Don says quickly, almost breathlessly.

"I will meet with Danielle there. See if our team leader thinks there is a way to get information from the Pentagon. I will take their high-speed train, Acela. It is the quickest way," Bob says.

"I'll get a team in place at Kings Bay," Don says.

They are silent for a few moments.

"Bob, you could be right. Keep recording what you see," Don says quietly.

"What do you mean?"

"Twenty-six-hundred warheads, that somehow the Americans believe are inadequate. With this country's history, these aren't gentler, smaller, or kinder. If another country finds out...well," He stops, shakes his head a bit, turning slightly, motioning with his hand at the traffic, "Gone in an instant."

Don puts the car in gear and pulls away from the curb, into the stream of traffic.

High above the streets, a Falcon dives towards a flight of pigeons. It reaches two hundred miles an hour as it plunges towards the pigeons flying frantically. The Falcon selects a white one. There is a puff of feathers as the talons dig in, which float in the sky, little bits of white, drifting, falling towards the street below.

The white feathers of the long-forgotten pigeon floating to the street below, falling at the feet of the pedestrians moving on the sidewalk, their eyes straight ahead, guns at the ready, the breathing units puffing to help them stay alive for another day.

Bob watches the feathers out the window, whispering, "Beautiful. So beautiful."

Road Trip

Fingers touch a screen on the dash of a car, the screen showing "9808 Mill, White Plains, New York" the car responds. A male voice says, "Good morning, John. 9808 Mill, E.T.A. four o'clock p.m."

"Here we go, Jack! New York city, 178 minutes." The car backs out of the driveway and eases into traffic.

"Nine million people, dad. Nine million—think of it. I am so excited to see the city." The boy looks at his dad, grinning, his right-hand flips in the air, his right knee bounces up and down as he talks. His body is in constant motion.

"You *should* be excited, Jack, this is your big adventure! So happy for you that we found this school. A good opportunity for you." John guides the car on to the ramp of the freeway and says, "Auto on." The voice responds, "Confirmed: auto on." John lets go of the wheel.

Jack's eyes are bright as the car moves with the traffic, "Look at all the cars, all of them are on auto. So many computer chips, radar, sensors, cameras all working constantly."

"Yes, so different than when I learned to drive. You had to learn how to park. I had a car that had a stick shift.

It was fun. I miss it. Not as much I will miss you this summer, though."

"This will be new for me, living with Mom. Living with someone is different than visiting. I am glad you worked out the visitation schedule. The school sounds different—I read all the material. They work with diverse types of children. It is their specialty. I hope I have positive experiences there. Last year I had some unpleasant ones."

Jack continues talking about Jack, "I hope I make friends at the new school. Having a girlfriend would be nice. Dad how do I get a girlfriend?"

"Be polite, be clean and you have to listen." John smiles as he says the word listen.

Jack is quiet for several miles, unusual for Jack.

"Dad, my erections are unexplainable. I mean, well, sometimes they are embarrassing."

John's smile is huge. "Jack De Falco, I was wondering how you would approach this subject. Your honesty...you make me smile. First you must make me a promise."

"What is the promise?"

"You have to listen—really listen—to what I'm saying."

As the car moves through traffic, John talks honestly about the human body, the joy of sex, and the responsibility that should go with it. He ends his talk with, "Millions of sperm are released, flying, seeking, then sometimes—sometimes—rarely one crashes into the female's egg. Infinity. Life. A miracle, Jack."

Jack's voice booms in the car, "Think of the image of that happening! Thank you, Dad, for talking to me about my erections! I can tell you are a theologian—the word 'infinity" in your explanation."

"Remember Jack, this is one of those subjects that you do not talk about in public, like armpit hair. Sometimes your honesty...well. it makes people uncomfortable."

"Ok, Dad."

The car maintains speed. John De Falco, smiling, makes the sign of the cross, giving thanks for the moment.

The city appears, the tops of the skyline hidden by smog. The screen on the car flashes an alert, "Air Quality Dangerous."

"The city is ahead, Jack."

Jack looks at the screen, "Yes. I see that. I wonder what the oxygen level is here?'

The car is silent as they enter heavy traffic. John grabs the wheel, "Auto off."

"I understand, Dad. I would not trust the auto drive with all of these cars either." John follows the instructions on the screen, safely navigating the throng of traffic. The voice announces, "You have arrived at 9808 Mill." John turns off the car.

"Jack, before we get out the car, give me a couple of moments to talk to you." Jack turns and looks at his dad.

"I have loved watching you this school year. Listening to you talk about your experiences at school. Wonderful moments, and yes, some embarrassing and even hurtful moments, too. Jack, here it is—this is what I want you to hear: There is no life without some pain. We all just must get through it. But you can call me anytime."

"Sure, dad, I will." With that they get Jack's roller bags out of the back of the car and walk up the sidewalk to the front door of the modest apartment. Grace is waiting at the front door.

John lets Jack take the lead, bringing up the rear. "Jack! Oh, Jack you've grown!" She gives him a hug. Jack, uncomfortable with affection, smiles, as always. "Hi, mom."

John looks at Grace, neckline plunging, hair curling, makeup perfect, as always. Always on display. He is still struck by her beauty, and struck harder by the pain of her infidelity. He is aware of his unease, his lack of confidence around her.

"Hi, John. How was the drive?" Grace too, feels she is not her usual smiling, confident self. With John, she was different. There was always this pain in between them. The makeup—the display—does nothing to fix it.

"Drive was ok. Jack and I had a good talk." John manages a smile.

"Mom, there were so many cars, and the air quality alert came on as we entered the city."

"This building has a particularly good filtering system. I've been sleeping well." Grace manages a smile of her own. "John, how is your position at the university going?"

"Good. I have full classes. Students are starting to reach out to me, worried about their future. I spend time listening to their concerns. And your job, Grace? How is your job?"

"I got my assignment today. I will be using all of what I have. It will be tough. Hope I can do it."

"Your IQ is off the charts; I am sure you can do this job Grace."

"IQ was never my problem." Graces face is solemn, her eyes flash to John, then they look down.

Jack breaks the tension, "Where should I put my stuff, mom?"

"Come on, Jack. Right down this hall." The three move down the hall and Grace opens the door. There is a nice desk and chair, bed, and set of drawers.

"Nice room, Jack. I see you have a nice place to study," John says.

"We'll take the subway for about ten minutes and then walk to school, and then I can walk to work from the school."

"Sounds good, Grace. I better get rolling. I have work tomorrow."

John puts his hand on Jack's shoulder, "Give me a call whenever you want to talk."

"Sure, dad."

"I will walk you out, John. Jack, you can start putting your clothes away."

The two head down the hallway, and out the door. Silence surrounds them as they walk. John leans up against the car, Grace glances away, their eyes do not lock. There is just the uncomfortable silence.

"Well, I better hit it. Have a good week. Let me know how the school is going with Jack."

"I will, John, I will. You be careful on the way back."

John, opens the car door, looking over the car at her. With no warning, she blurts out, "We can communicate about Jack. Why not...why not *us*?"

John stands there, the door open, still unsure, afraid. He nods his head, "Maybe. Maybe..." is all that comes out of his mouth. He swings into the car, shuts the door, and drives away.

— 6 —

The Friendship Begins

Jack De Falco wakes early, rolls out of bed, and heads towards the bathroom, his hands covering the bump in his red boxer shorts. He is eleven years old, a little under five feet tall, one hundred pounds dripping wet, and has black hair always combed straight back; you can see he is going to be a handsome man. He glances down the hallway to see his mother quickly turn away as he enters.

"Good morning, Jack," she says, a smile on her lips. There is no answer, just sound of the stool flushing. Jack emerges from the bathroom and walks over to his mother by the coffee maker, sipping her coffee. "Your first day in New York!"

"Yes, my first day in New York, my first day at summer school. I am excited, nervous, and hopeful at the same time. 'Endless Possibilities' is the name of the school. Why did they name it that?" His right-hand flips rapidly as he talks, his loud voice animated.

He doesn't meet Grace's eyes, but she's used to it. Grace looks at her son, the black hair, eye lashes, dark eyes—almost black. *So handsome*, she thinks, then says,

"I don't know Jack. It's a good question to ask. A good *first* question to ask."

"I am sure I will have other questions," he says. His voice booms in the quiet apartment.

"Yes, I am sure you will, Jack. I have your cereal on the table; get dressed. Then, get ready to roll. Your first day in New York and the first day to ride the Metro."

Jack dresses, then returns and pours some milk on the cereal and sits down. He grabs a spoon, holding it in his fist, and takes a huge bite of cereal. A little bit of milk dribbles out of the corner of his mouth.

"Slow down a little bit. You have plenty of time," Grace chuckles, "I'm going to get ready."

Jack nods his head and continues to shovel into the cereal. His right knee bounces some as he eats and stares straight ahead, eyes wide. "I wonder what today will be like," he says to no one.

Soon, they walk out the door of the modest apartment building and down the sidewalk. Grace's hair is tied back; she walks quickly with ease, sometimes reaching down and touching her boy on the shoulder.

"This'll be a good day, Jack. You get to see how I go to work and learn how to get on the Metro. It's so good to have you this summer."

Jack looks at her. "I am excited to be in New York City. I am glad that you and dad worked out the visitation schedule. It is so different from the country. So many people. Over nine million. Think, mom, over nine million people." He adds, somewhat unnecessarily, "I like numbers and data. Numbers, data, facts. I like numbers and data." His hand flips at the wrist as he talks.

Jack is dressed in blue jeans, white tennis shoes, and a T-shirt with the symbol pi. He walks like it is difficult, toes touching the sidewalk first.

"I like numbers and data. Numbers and data are real." The hands flutter rapidly, emphasizing the repetition of his statement. "Numbers and data are real."

"Yes, Jack, I know," Grace answers, then gently adds, "Remember to keep working on not repeating your phrases. Some people may be bothered by it."

"Sometimes I cannot help it, mom. It is who I am! It is who I am!" Jack looks at his mother with his brows furrowed.

Grace stops walking for a moment, placing a hand on her son's arm. "We all have something that makes us different, all of us. Your father, your doctors, me. All of us. Now, remember what your doctor said: breathe when you finish a thought. Then speak."

"I will try, I will try. I am happy to be here in New York this summer. So happy that you and Dad worked out the visitation schedule. We had a good visit on our way here yesterday," he replies, looking down at his shoes.

"Good, I'm glad you had time to talk. Nothing like a little road trip."

"Yes, I talked to him about my puberty issues. He listened well. He said my erections were completely natural, completely natural. That they are a good thing," Jack smiles, making rare eye contact with his bright eyes.

"I'm…glad you talked to your father about this," Grace's face grows hot with discomfort.

"I thought there was something wrong with me. Sometimes, they just happen with no warning!"

Grace walks faster as if trying to escape the blush on her face.

"Dad said he was shy growing up. Had acne and few friends. He said I have many advantages. That I will be fine. That my Asperger's, ADHD, and all the rest are a strength. He said that I would make new friends here," Jack continues, his voice louder this time at the thought of the opportunities. "Having a girl for a friend would be nice. Mom, what do girls like? Can you tell me what I should do? How do I get a girlfriend?"

They walk on and stop at a pedestrian crossing, waiting for the light to change.

"Let me see...Listen. Be polite. Behavior is important. Be clean," Grace replies, relieved that the conversation is less embarrassing.

"That is what Dad said. Is it that easy? Is that all I do to have a girlfriend? I am clean now, I am polite, and I listen. Why don't I have a girlfriend?"

"You're only eleven years old! There is plenty of time for girls. Come on, let's go up to the corner. I'll get a cup of coffee, you can grab a donut, and we'll get on the Metro," Grace says, and they start walking again.

"Yes, it is my first day in the city. In New York, I am one of more than nine million people. Nine million. I like numbers. Numbers and data are real!" Jack's hand flips rapidly.

Grace jumps in before he can get stuck in a repetition cycle again. "Breathe with me Jack, and listen to the city." She gestures. "Look up at the skyscrapers. The wind came in last night; the air has cleared, so we can see the sun!"

Jack absently stops flipping his hand as he looks up at the skyscrapers. "Sunrise, sunlight hitting everything. The earth is turning, orbiting our sun, ninety-three million miles away. The sun is not rising at all." Grace smiles at him as he looks up, bright eyes watching the sun hit the tops of the buildings. Then he looks out at the traffic.

"How many cars are moving in this city as the earth turns. How many?"

Grace sighs, shaking her head as he continues to repeat himself, watching the cars go by. His hand flipping starts again as he repeats, "How many, how many?"

"Come on, Jack," Grace sighs, a bit of impatience in her voice. They walk on and come around the corner to Sam's kiosk. He gives his usual friendly smile and greeting while wiping down his workspace.

Sam's smile widens as he recognizes her. "Ah, good to see you again, Grace! How about that sunshine? The wind brought in some new air! What can I get you this morning?"

"Good to see you too, Sam. This is my son, Jack. Jack, this is Sam. He has great coffee, and I'll bet even better donuts," Grace says, smiling to herself at the fact he remembered her name.

"One coffee, and how many donuts does this young man, Jack, need today?" Sam asks, leaning over the counter to get a better look at the boy.

"I would like two, please, and an apple juice!" Jack booms back.

Sam assembles the items and places all of them on the counter. As he's doing so, Bob steps up behind Grace.

"Morning, Bob. Give me a moment," Sam says over Grace's shoulder. Grace turns around to see him.

"You're the man that saved me yesterday. Thank you again!"

"You are most welcome. It was simply a person who thought someone else's property would help them," Bob replied.

Turning to Jack, Grace explains, "A young man tried to steal my purse yesterday. This man," she turns back to Bob, "I'm sorry, I don't know your name?"

"Bob. Bob Goeman."

"Bob Goeman, I am Grace De Falco. This is my son, Jack."

"Grace, Jack, good to meet you," Bob says, looking intently at them both.

As Grace explains yesterday's events, Jack looks at Bob wide-eyed. Turning back to Grace, he says, "An act of extreme desperation. That kid couldn't have known how much money you had in your purse. How would he evaluate the possible gain versus the risk? What kind of data did he have to attempt the theft? How desperate must he have been to take such extreme risk?"

Jack seems to play the scene in his head as he talks. Bob steps closer to Jack, listening intently to him speak.

"Yes. You ask important questions, Jack. He is starving, yet he did not ask for help. He was trying to stay alive," Bob's tone is affirmative. He looks directly at Jack, studying his fidgeting movements of wrist flicking and the way he looks at the ground when speaking or being spoken to.

Sam pauses the conversation to say, "Ok, we have talked about how desperate you've got to be to try and steal a woman's purse. How about the donuts and coffee? Bob, you want your usual?"

"Yes, please," Bob says.

Grace and Jack gather up their order and move out of the way.

"What are you photographing today?" Grace asks.

"I am taking the Metro-North. Arlington, The Pentagon. Just trying to do a piece on that area. Such an interesting place," Bob replies.

"We are taking the Metro-North. This will be my first time riding the subway!" Jack says excitedly, donut crumbs already gathering around his mouth.

"What do we owe you today?" Grace asks Sam as she digs through her purse.

"Thirty dollars for all," Sam replies.

She shuffles until she pulls out a crisp fifty-dollar bill and hands it to Sam, who grins widely.

"Here you go," she says with a smile. Sam starts to count the change to give back to her, but she shakes her head and puts up a hand to stop him. "Keep it. Have a good day."

Bob sees the fifty-dollar bill on the counter, the generosity. He sees Sam's smile growing even more prominent on his sweaty face, and remembers her saying, 'I would have given him money if he had asked.'

"You and Jack have a good day together," Sam says with one hand resting on his heart and the other wiping a bead of sweat off his forehead.

With that, they start walking towards the subway. It's as if they had known each other forever, Bob gliding alongside Grace, whose posture is perfect. Jack walks between them, wolfing down his second donut, gulping the juice, and finishing it all in a couple of minutes. At the stairway entrance to the subway, Bob slips in front of the two.

"Jack, stay between your mother and me," he says. With that, they enter the morning herd of people.

"Tunnels; how many miles of tunnels are there in New York City? How many people move through these tunnels every day? How did they make them? Are all these people good people? Will any of them harm us or try to steal from us?" Jack asks. Bob looks at him and nods his head in agreement.

"As you can tell, Jack is always asking questions," Grace says somewhat nervously.

Bob replies, "People will learn too when they find the answers to his questions. Questions, asking 'Why?' is so important."

"So, you think my questions are important?" Jack asks.

"Of course they are. You are seeking data. Questions are important. Keep asking questions."

Jack's smile grows. Bob's eyes focus on him as they walk to the boarding platform. Grace glances around, looking at the other pedestrians, searching for a familiar face.

"Who are you looking for?" Bob asks, seeing her behavior.

"Oh. It's nothing. I just met a homeless man yesterday after almost losing my purse. I told him I'd see him today. I hope he's ok. There was something about him."

"Interesting that you befriended a homeless person after the way your morning began."

"I was feeling thankful."

"Did you get the name of this person?"

"Yes. Billy."

"Billy?"

"Yes, why?"

"I met a homeless person yesterday, and his name was "Billy."

"Out of nine million, what is the probability that you met the same person?" Jack asks. Grace shrugs, unsure how to answer such a question. Bob smiles at Jack, nodding approval at his question.

The train finally arrives. Most people waiting shine with perspiration, their faces void of expression in the heat and foul air with breathing units puffing.

Jack looks at the rails below and shouts as a giant rat runs by. Grace smiles and lets out a small laugh at her son's excitement.

"Rattus norvegicus. There are over thirty-nine million in New York City. How much food do you think is being thrown away by people to feed thirty-nine million rats?" Grace asks.

"Why is so much food being thrown away?" Bob repeats musingly.

"Most people are afraid of rats. People are not feeding them on purpose. People do not consume all the food they purchase. The rat consumes most of the food we throw away. Miscellaneous insects and maggots if enough time passed. Then the flies, of course, cycle," Jack answers excitedly.

"Excellent observation. You see so much that others do not," Bob says. Jack beams, nodding at the man, thrilled with the affirmation. Grace looks back and forth between them as if she cannot believe the conversation; how quickly Bob and Jack have become friends. The train enters the station, and the noise stops the conversation.

After a few seconds, Jack booms, his voice loud enough to be heard over the train, "The British hired Hessian mercenaries in 1776 to fight in the American revolutionary war. The mercenaries unknowingly brought the Norway rat with them in their grain's stores on the ships. Think of what the British decision to hire mercenaries did. Millions of rats here."

Bob looks at him. "That is an amazing memory you have."

Jack smiles, his hand flipping slows. "I remember most of what I read," he says.

The three enter a train car. Grace takes the window seat, Jack in the middle, and Bob, in the aisle. Jack's head is moving around, taking in everything. His eyes light up with joy.

As the train starts to move, Grace asks, "So, what will you be taking pictures of at Arlington or the Pentagon."

"I am not sure. I cannot take any pictures inside the Pentagon, of course, and Arlington Cemetery is a sad place. 400,000 graves. I am unsure if I will take any pictures at all," Bob said.

"400,000 graves?" Jack said, his voice dropping in volume and his face suddenly sullen. No one responds, and the three are silent for a while.

Grace breaks the silence. "So, Bob, are you a professional photographer?"

"Professional photographer? I take many pictures that represent the places I find myself in. I enjoy documenting what I see.

Grace asks, "Why the 'Rattus Norvegicus?'"

"Any living thing on this planet, I am interested in. Rattus Norvegicus thrives on what another species is throwing away. Not having to be stressed about their food, shelter, or tomorrow. I am sure they are happier than most humans," Bob replies.

"Happy? You think rats have emotions?" Grace asks.

"Yes."

Jack jumps in, "You took pictures of a rat?"

"Yes, I did."

"May I see, please?" Jack responds.

Bob looks at Grace, who nods.

"Show him the one where it's got pepperoni," she smiles, thinking about their first interaction.

Bob pulls the camera out and thumbs through the images. "Here you are. Toggle that button, and it will go forward." He demonstrates, moving the button back and forth a few times.

Jack's small hands take the camera and scroll through the rat pictures, examining them thoroughly. "Is that pepperoni?" he asks and points to the image.

Bob smiles, "Yes, it is. I love pepperoni."

"And those are... "Jack trails off, looking closer to the camera again, eyes squinting to get a better look.

Bob takes the camera to examine the picture he is looking at.

"Those are the female Rattus mammary glands. Which means she is nursing her young. She is one of the thousands of mammal species on this little blue dot," Bob says.

Grace listens to the conversation, the back and forth between her son and this strange man. Bob is totally focused on Jack; she can tell that Jack loves how he listens to every word he says.

"She has babies; she is a mother. She is a warm-blooded mammal like us, and she nurses her young. I bet they love their mother. I can see them all curled up with her nursing," Jack says, excitedly shaking his hands at the thought of the babies.

"You are correct; she is a mammal. We could assume if she made it back to her young that morning, they would have been hungry and glad to have her back," Bob explains.

"You mean happy, right?" Jack asks.

"Yes."

"Thank you for showing me the picture," Jack says happily, returning the camera to the man.

"Our stop is up ahead," Grace says to Jack, "Do you have any more questions for Bob?" She gathers her things together.

"Yes, I do. Bob, do you have a son? Will you be riding the subway again? We will be riding the subway every day this summer," Jack says.

"I do not have a son. Yes, I am sure I will be riding the subway again," Bob replies, tucking his camera away.

Jack looks at his mother silently, and Grace's face softens. "Mr. Goeman, do you have a card or something with a phone number? It's a rare to find someone patient enough to have that kind of conversation with Jack. You really listen."

Jack adds, "Maybe we could all ride the subway together!" His grin bursts across his face.

Bob smiles, "Let me check in my bag." He rustles around and brings out a battered card:

Bob Goeman
Freelance Photographer
914-835-8090

"Thank you, Mr. Goeman," Grace says and takes the card.

Over the speaker comes an announcement, "White Plains, New York, next stop."

"That's us." To Jack, Grace adds, "You get to see where I work before you go to school."

"My mother is an engineer. She works at Parabola Systems. She is brilliant. She designs-"

"Jack, enough about me," Grace interrupts quickly. Her face is losing its softness.

The train stops, and Bob stands up to let them out. "Grace, Jack, you two have a wonderful day. I hope your first day of school goes well."

"Hope I get to see you again, Bob Goeman!" Jack says, loud enough for all to hear.

Bob sits back down. As he does, a man stops beside him, "Hey, asshole, found anything to eat dumpster-diving lately?"

Bob looks up; the man who was at the door in the alley walks by, still dressed neatly in his suit and tie, the bulge of the holster showing at his hip as he moves with a walk that says, 'get out of my way.' When the man exits the train, Bob looks out the window to see him follow Grace and Jack.

His concentration breaks when his phone begins to ring and vibrate in his pocket. He answers it swiftly.

"Good morning, Don. I am still on the train. Can this wait? I must make the Acela connection. I will be in Arlington in about three hours." Bob leans forward to continue watching the man follow Grace and Jack. They fade from view as the train leaves the station.

Bob leans back in his seat, his face, usually free of emotion, tightens. He closes his eyes, his lips moving silently.

Boy Meets Girl

Grace and Jack exit the train with the crowd of commuters, accompanied by the sounds of thousands of shoes on the cement floor, the movement of the people, and the puffing of breathing units. The people, their eyes straight ahead, don't talk to each other, try to breathe, and make it to work another day.

Jack is the exception. His head turns rapidly, scanning the crowd of people, his voice booming out over the crowd. "Why are they all so quiet? No one is talking. Look at all of them! I have never seen so many people in one place. Mom, it reminds me of the National Geographic special on wildebeests in Africa. Their migration. Remember Mom?" His head turned rapidly, looking at the crowd; some of the people are staring at him.

Grace looks at her son, and the throng of people, many of them looking at Jack. She shakes her head, "Yes, Jack, there are many people. Please try not to be so loud."

"Ok," he says before immediately diving on, "They do remind me of the wildebeests. The plastic on their nose and mouth makes them look strange. How far is my school from where you work? I am feeling some apprehension about the school. On my first day, I will not know anyone. Does the school have a filtration system? The air is much worse here than at Dad's."

Grace touches Jack's shoulder. "Jack, I spent some time yesterday with the instructor you'll be with this morning. Her name is Ms. Alana. I was impressed! You'll be fine, a lot of freedom with what you want to work on, study, or read. And yes, it was easy to breathe in the school. It's only a short walk from work, which is fortunate for both of us."

They walk on Main Street to the Parabola Systems building. Grace says, "This is where I work. I'll get permission someday to take you in for a quick tour. Still, the security is strict."

"How come?"

Grace answers, "Parabola Systems designs and builds military systems. They want to keep information about those systems secret."

Jack counters, "You mean weapons."

Grace sighs. "It's best to just tell you I'm an engineer at Parabola Systems."

"You mean you cannot tell me? Is it a secret?"

"Correct. A secret." She smiles. "If they ask, tell people I'm an engineer."

"So, your job requires lots of computation?"

"Yes. For the first time, I have a job where I'll get to use my mathematical abilities."

Jack, for the first time, is silent as they approach the school building.

Grace is in the lead as they walk up to the school. The sign above says 'Endless Possibilities.' Caricatures of children on the sign hold hands. Grace walks forward, Jack slightly behind her, trailing, his hand flipping anxiously.

Noticing this, Grace turns to him and says, "Jack, look at me. What did your doctor tell you to do when you're anxious?"

Jack's forehead is strained, a light coat of sweat covering it. "Breathe deeply and think of what I am inside. Visualize all of me, my cells, the neurons firing, so many of them, so many, a miracle."

"Good. Let's do that together." She stands still, breathing slowly as she instructs him. "Just breathe."

Jack stands with her for a few minutes, taking deep, steady breaths. Then Grace puts her hand on his shoulder. "Let's go inside now. This is your adventure."

They walk along the side of the building, the cameras pan, following them.

"Look, Mom, look at all the cameras," Jack points.

"They have the newest facial recognition system," she says, then adds, "You've been filmed and remembered."

Jack smiles. "I am still anxious but better."

With that, they walk up to the door.

Herschel's voice calls a greeting from behind the desk, "Good morning! You must be Jack. Welcome to your first day!"

Jack looks at Grace hesitantly and says, "Yes, I am Jack De Falco."

"Miss De Falco, welcome back." The door clicks, and Herschel swings it open. Jack and Grace step in.

Jack looks up at this huge man. His chest is twice as big as Jack's own, standing solidly a foot above him. Jack's hand flips lightly.

Herschel gets down on one knee, roughly eye level with Jack. Jack sees the gun strapped to his belt. "Hi, Jack. I'm Herschel Thompson. My job is to greet you all and keep everyone safe. Your guide will be here in a minute. I'm so happy for you, and I'm sure you will love this school."

Jack manages a smile, nodding a bit before a soft female voice says from behind him, "Good Morning! My name is Lola McGregor. I'm gonna show you around."

Jack turns and looks at the girl standing in front of him. Five feet, maybe 110 lbs., her light brown hair tied back by a yellow ribbon, and just a dab of red on her lips.

She speaks again. "What's your name?" Jack struggles to find his voice, his eyes cast downward, but Lola just smiles. She takes a step closer to him, her bright brown eyes looking directly at him, head cocked to one side. "Kid? What's your name?"

Finally, Jack manages a smile, his dark eyes meet hers, and he stammers, "My name…my name is Jack." Now that he's started, he can't quit staring and smiling at the girl. His hands stop shaking, and his voice comes out softer, more confident. "Jack De Falco."

"Jack De Falco," Lola says with a nod. "Let's go look at our school."

Jack turns to his mother a final time, smile still huge. Grace motions for him to go, shooing her hands and waving. With that, Jack and Lola start down the hall.

When they're out of sight, Grace turns to Herschel, her lip quivering just a bit. Herschel looks at her and simply says, "Go ahead." She covers her mouth and choked back a sob. Then for some reason, she reaches up and touches his shoulder.

After she composes herself, Grace turns to go. Herschel walks with her. They are both quiet.

Herschel speaks first. "I've watched these so many times, but each time I remember my first day at school. I stumbled around, trying to find my room. I knew I was going to be the biggest kid in class. The rest of the kids thought I had been held back, that I was stupid. It would have been easier if someone had been with me when I walked into that room. The silence…one girl giggled; the rest stared. I remember it like yesterday. I think Jack will remember this day, but he'll do it with a smile. God, I love this job."

"I am so glad you are here for these children," Grace says. She can't think of a better response.

"Thank you, Miss De Falco."

"Just call me Grace."

Herschel's eyes twinkle, and he beams, "Grace. Have a wonderful day at work. This is your first day, too, right?

"Yes, yes, it is. I'm walking there now. Thanks again, Herschel," she says and gives him a slight wave.

As she walks away, she sees a man approaching the school. A girl walks by his side, holding his hand. She holds some of her hair in her hand, chewing on it.

Grace stops to watch the pair walk up to the school. The scene repeats; Herschel greets the girl, getting down to her level while she continues to chew her hair. Grace can just hear him saying, "Good morning, Laura! Welcome to your first day! I'm Herschel. Your guide will be here in a minute." With Hershel's warm smile to reassure her, the girl slowly lets the hair drop from her mouth. Her father beams.

Grace walks away, remembering the conversation with Ms. Alana.

"Our job is to send these children into the world, knowing who they are. Their strengths, their weaknesses. With the way the world is now, we need these children."

She takes several deep breaths as she walks, glancing at the cameras that are panning, turning, following her. She rubs her face again with her hand and looks at it. There is nothing on it, just the air, the dirty air.

— 8 —

Jack's First Day

Lola and Jack walk down the hallway of the school together. Jack's toes touch the tiled floor first, then his heels follow suit, coming down with a hard strike as his right hand occasionally flips in the air. Lola pays no mind to his movements.

"Where do you live?" Lola asks.

Jack looks at her with eyes wide as he walks along. His hand flipping slows when she looks at him. "I am here for the summer. We live in Westchester." His voice is still loud with nerves, but Lola doesn't seem to notice.

"I live in Mamaroneck," Lola replies.

"The history of your town is interesting," says Jack immediately, louder with enthusiasm as he tells her the facts he once read. "It was purchased from Chief Wappaquewam by John Richbell. I think in 1661."

Lola stops walking and looks at Jack, surprised. "How do you know that?"

"I like data, numbers, and interesting history. I remember most of what I read. I find it interesting that Na-

tive Americans could sell something they had never purchased." Jack's smile widens at her interest.

"That is interesting, Jack, and you remembered all
that," Lola says.

They turn a corner and start down another hallway.
There is a pause in the conversation as Lola checks the
room numbers.

"My mother says my talking sometimes upsets people," blurts Jack, "Most people may find it annoying that I
talk about numbers, interesting history."

Lola laughs, "Jack, it's fine. I like your facts; now,
when people ask me where I live, I can tell them I live where
Chief Wappaquewam used to live." Enamored in three minutes, Jack stares at her as his hand stop flipping.

Lola finally finds the door she wants and walks
through, Jack following. In the center of the room are chairs
arranged in a large circle. Several students are already sitting. At the front of the group sits a middle-aged woman
with a big, welcoming smile.

"Good morning, Lola," The woman says and, turning to Jack, adds, "And I'm betting this is Jack De Falco.
Welcome to your first day! My name is Alana Corcoran,
but you can call me Ms. Alana. You may sit anywhere you
want to. Lola, thank you for bringing him here. Do you
have anything to share about Jack that you learned on
your walk here?"

"Yes! He lives in Westchester. He loves data, numbers,
and interesting history – so I learned this morning that I
live where Chief Wappauquewam used to live. Jack knew
that!" Lola explains, grinning still.

"Jack, you have a memory I would like to have," Alana
says to the boy approvingly.

"I like interesting history," Jack says, voice quieter
than before.

Alana gestures to the circle of chairs. "Please, have a seat. Lola, thank you again."

Jack's smile has disappeared. His hand is flipping again, his breathing rapid. The room suddenly feels too large, and all eyes are watching him. Jack turns back to Lola, who is now by the classroom door.

"Enjoy your class, Jack!" Lola waves at him as she leaves.

Jack takes a chair. His foot and knee start shaking and bouncing as he looks around at the others in the circle. The only thing he can focus on is the sound of his teacher's voice .

"Well, now that everyone's here, let's get started. As you all know, school officially started last week, but due to scheduling, you all couldn't make it. So, I get to do this with you! This is my favorite class; we call it Relax. Now is when I learn about you, so let's start by just taking turns saying who we are and something about ourselves. Who would like to start?"

Silence and tension fill the space between the six students in the circle. Jack's knee is bouncing. He looks at the others, waiting for someone to speak; one girl picks her nose, a boy scratches his arm viciously, another boy looks at the floor, a larger girl chews on her hair, a very skinny girl taps the desk with her pencil. The only sound in the room is the tap, tap of the pencil.

Finally, Jack blurts, 'There is something wrong with all of us.' Realizing what he's said, he looks up, expecting Ms. Alana to reprimand him, but sees her smiling instead. Slightly panicked, he continues, "My name is Jack, Jack De Falco. I like numbers, data, and history."

"Thank you for starting," Ms. Alana says, voice calm. She touches her chest with folded hands, eyes shining. "You made my heart happy. Who will be next to tell Jack De Falco and Ms. Alana who you are?"

One at a time, they all say their names; some even manage to say something about themselves. Ms. Alana nodded each time, touching her chest as if in prayer, "Thank you. You made my heart happy too."

The boy looking at the floor is glancing at others in the room. The pencil is no longer tapping, the arm scratching, nose picking, and hair chewing have stopped, and Jack's knee is still again. Ms. Alana looks at all the children and smiles, "This is my favorite day, your first day."

Nine Million Homo Sapiens

Grace leaves the school and walks back toward Parabola Systems. She looks up at a billboard and sees an advertisement for Tesla's newest car, with Elon Musk beside it. She stands still for a few moments, remembering the interview.

• • •

"Elon Musk! Wow, Elon Musk. I read your entire profile last night. You worked with Elon Musk!" the man in front of her said, not hiding his excitement whatsoever. "Sorry, Ms. De Falco, I am Wayne Findley. I got caught up in reading this."

A dark-haired man with a peppering of grey sat behind a large wooden desk. On the wall was a picture of a Titan missile in the air. Some crow's feet showed around his eyes, thick glasses perched on his nose, and a small gold St. Christopher pendant on top of the well-pressed blue shirt. He took a sip of coffee out of his cup. "Coffee, Grace? May I call you Grace?"

"Yes, on both counts," Grace's left knee bounced, so she placed her hand on it as Wayne got up and went to the coffee bar.

"Anything in it?"

"Just sugar. Four, if you don't mind."

Wayne chuckled. "Four sugars, got it. I love it too." He brought her the coffee in a mug and continued, "I hate paper cups. Coffee always tastes better from a real cup."

She took the coffee in her right hand, keeping her left on her knee, then started, "Yes, I worked with SpaceX and Mr. Musk on several of their projects. A multiple-payload launch was the last project I worked on. Computing the orbits. I liked the problem-solving and the fact that I was working with everyone, from kids fresh out of college to people from all over the world. Brilliant, all of them. Amazing people."

"What brings you to Parabola Systems?"

"A...change in the family. Divorce. I grew up here, so I decided to come back, and my son is on the spectrum, so I wanted to ensure he had the resources he needed. There's some wonderful help for him here."

"You would leave Space X for your son?"

"Yes."

"Why?"

Grace blinked. "Jack requires some special education accommodations. I'd like to be able to provide that for him."

"How old is Jack?"

"Eleven. Jack is asking me about why he does not have a girlfriend."

Wayne chuckled, "Enjoy the questions. They will become fond memories." Then he continues more seriously, "Grace, your credentials, what you've done, could be a perfect fit for what we need. That being said, some of what we do is military and highly classified. Would you have a problem with working on weapon systems?"

She took a moment before responding. "At Space X, some of the satellites we launched were dubbed 'communication.' We knew that meant we would never know what they did. We just hoped they were not listening to us. Weapon systems mean the actual device if used, would kill people. That's your real question. Am I correct?"

Wayne's face was solemn. "Yes. There's no sugar-coating it; many of our systems are designed for that. The way I see it, I hope it deters someone from trying anything against us. I push you on this because we have had people resign because they are working on weapons that would destroy an entire city."

Grace nodded. "Mr. Findley, I would like to think I lived in a world where everyone plays fair. I do not think that way. I could work on your systems."

"The other thing I want you to consider is that this will be a lifelong decision on your part, even if you're only here for a short time. You'll be asked to sign away certain rights to privacy to work here. I will send you away with a document that you will need to sign. Please feel free to have your attorney look at it. In a nutshell, the company can look at your financial and social life at any time."

"Trying to prevent spying, I assume?" Grace asked.

"Yes." Wayne handed her a manilla envelope. "The compensation package is in there, too," he added.

"Thank you, Mr. Findley."

"Call me Wayne. We will check you out and let you know. This will take several weeks."

A month later, she checked her messages at the Space X testing center in McGregor, Texas. "Please call Wayne Findley. We have an offer for you."

"Mr. Findley, Grace De Falco. I am listening... Oh, yes, Yes! Thank you! I will take the job. How soon do you want me there?"

. . .

Grace walks past the billboard, down Cypress Street, to the Parabola Systems building. She enters through gleaming revolving doors and watches the marble floors shine in front of her as she walks through the large foyer. Two security officers stand in front of the elevators by a glass booth that looks like a scanner at an airport.

Standing there with them is Wayne Findley. He smiles and says, "Good Morning, Grace."

She looks at him, and sees the gold, small St. Christopher medal on the blue shirt. "Good morning, Mr. Findley."

"Wayne," he corrects, "We're on a first-name basis here. Nervous people don't create well, so we want our people to relax." Wayne's deep, Texan drawl is soft, each vowel clear. He turns to the security men. "Patrick, Brock, this is Grace De Falco." Both men nod at her.

"Welcome to your first day, Grace," says the one Wayne had pointed out as Richard. "Just put your phone and any personal items in the tray and step in the booth." Grace does so, and he continues, "Raise your arms up, just like in an airport." The machine circles her several times. "Ok, step on out." She gathers her personal items out of the tray.

"Tomorrow," says Wayne, "I'll go into detail about the security here, but I'm behind this morning. Still, I want to make sure you understand the necessity."

"It's fine, Mr. Findley...ah, Wayne," says Grace, "That was easier than a pat down at the airport."

They proceed to the elevators. Wayne pushes the button, and the doors close. "I'll explain in detail tomorrow how that machine works," he repeats, "It's higher tech than the airport. Today, I wanted to get you busy. Make it on the subway, okay? Get Jack to school, all right?"

"Yes. A lovely girl greeted him, and I swear I thought Jack would smile so wide it'd break into pieces. She was so sincere and kind. Jack forgot I was there." Realizing she's rambling, Grace finishes, "Endless Possibilities, it's called. It's close to here."

Wayne nods. "Several of our people have children in that school. Amazing work with children. I hear people talking about it all the time. So, a girl started Jack's first day!" Wayne chuckles, thinking of their interview.

"He was so anxious as we got closer and closer to the school. Then they had this girl meet him to take him to his first class. She calmed him right down. It was heartwarming to watch."

Wayne laughs deeply, "How wonderful! Nothing like two young people getting along. Get settled in ok otherwise? Did our realtor associate take good care of you?"

"Yes, thank you for your help. Just what I needed: close to the subway, in a safe area." After a pause, she says, "Speaking of safety, could you do me a favor?" Wayne pauses, listening. "I know you have a security team here." She reaches into her wallet, takes out a card, and hands it to Wayne. "This man stopped a theft yesterday, and saved my purse and pride. He connected with Jack in twenty minutes on the subway. He listened to Jack in a way I had never experienced, and Jack would like to see him again. If it wouldn't be too much to ask, would you get me some information about him? Not a dossier or anything like that. Just basic things."

Wayne takes the card, looks at it, and says, "Anything for you and Jack. I'll give you something by tomorrow."

The elevator stops, the doors open, and Wayne and Grace enter the hallway. They walk until they come to an office with "Grace De Falco" on a plaque on the door. "Here you are. This is yours," says Wayne as he takes a magnetic card out of his shirt pocket and slips it in the door. There is a click. He hands her the card.

Wayne swings open the door to reveal a large room, sunlight streaming through large windows on the opposite wall. On the west wall is a large dry-erase board, and a large computer screen takes up the east wall. A desk with a computer sits in front of the large screen.

Grace smiles, "This is so nice. There's plenty of room for thinking. I like the dry-erase board – I prefer it for working formulas. I like to stand back and look at the equations. Your people have thought of everything." She takes a deep breath. "The air is wonderful here! How do you do that?"

"Glad you like it. Yes, we tweak the atmosphere in the building. The oxygen level is twenty-one percent, where it should be rather than the level it is outside." As she settles in, he continues, "You'll get a folder on a project that just started. It has to do with payloads and changing how they react to reentry; it fits your expertise to a tee. Coffee room right down the hall, and if you need something, I'm here. Welcome aboard, Grace."

Wayne turns and heads out of the room. As he does, a young man with a small flat metal box appears at the door. "Good morning, Wayne. Is this Miss De Falco?"

Wayne replies, "Morning, Max. Yes, it is. Do you have her folder?"

He nods. "I just need her card." Grace offers it and Max takes Grace's card, puts it in a handheld scanner, then hands it back with a small stylus. "Just sign the screen there with this, confirming you got the folder." She signs the screen. The box makes a clicking sound, and Max opens it and hands her a folder, then holds out his hand. "Oh, yes— your phone? It will be at security where you checked in. First, just put this number in for forwarding. If you have a call, it will ring here in your office. "

Grace puts the phone number in, and hands him the phone. "Thanks, Max. Are you new here, too? "

"Been here a month. I'm an intern; learning the ropes. Nice people. Love it."

"Thanks, Max. I'll see what I am working on. I'm excited to get started."

Grace shuts the door behind Max and Wayne, lays the folder on the table, then goes to the windows and looks out. The view of the city is spectacular; the sun shining from the windows all around her looks like a sparkling sea.

She turns and goes to her desk to open the folder. The first page, in bold letters, reads, "NEW REQUIREMENTS FOR THE TRIDENT II MISSILE SYSTEM: 2,600 WARHEADS.

"Decrease payload from 101kg to 90kg per multiple reentry vehicles, (i.e., sixteen per Trident) total kg decrease of 176 kg. Calculation for new burn times and altitude requirements for targeting due to new reentry and glide path parameters."

Grace gets up and goes to the south window again. She watches the cars, the people on the sidewalk, and the city skyline that goes on forever.

"Nine million Homo sapiens," she mutters aloud.

— 10 —

Those Who Follow Orders

"Arlington Station, next stop." The voice over the intercom wakes Bob up. He gathers his camera bag and moves down the aisle to exit with the others.

As he walks away from the train, he pulls out his phone. "Good morning, Don. The woman who almost had her purse stolen was at Sam's coffee this morning with her son Jack. We may have a new way of accessing data."

There is a pause.

"Because she works at Parabola Systems; she is an engineer. Parabola Systems is the builder of the Ohio Class Nuclear submarine, the Launch platform for the Trident nuclear missile."

Bob listens for some time and then talks again.

"The man at the dumpster is following her, so we must assume she knows something. Her background indicates she would be doing computations for missile loads and targeting. Others may think Grace knows what the warheads are being changed to. We must be the first to get the data. I will contact you later tonight. Hopefully, our team members will have data from the White House. I wonder if I am being followed. If he did see me, he only knows me as a homeless asshole. I will be more observant."

He hangs up and puts the phone in his pocket, his face growing heavy with concern. He turns around as if lost, scanning the people around him before he walks to the street and hails a cab.

"Where to?" the driver asks as he slides into the back seat.

"Arlington National Cemetery, please," Bob replies.

"You got it." The driver pulls away from the curb and enters the traffic. "Have you visited there before?"

"No," Bob replies quickly.

The driver looks in the mirror. "No family, next of kin there?"

"No. I just wanted to see it."

The car stops at a traffic light. The driver, still looking in the mirror, notes Bob looking out the window at the crowded streets.

"I've never been there," he says, "I thought about taking the wife and kid there. I've taken a lot of fares there, but we've never gone. We did go to the shopping mall, right next to Arlington. It's amazing. So big! You might check that out, too."

The car moves again as the light changes.

"I do not need to purchase anything," Bob says, then asks, "What did you purchase at this shopping mall?"

"My wife bought a lot of clothes - you know, women. My boy bought a video game, *Last Battle*. My boy and I play it together. Awesome game. Great graphics."

"I have never experienced playing a video game. Please explain," Bob asks, and the driver perks up.

"You've never played? In this one, you choose a side, pick your weapons, and then fight enemies. You really get immersed in the game. It's...I dunno, exhilarating."

"How do you win this game?" Bob asks, now invested in the idea of this *Last Battle*.

"You've really never played a video game, have you?" The driver chuckles.

"No, I have not."

"You win the round by getting all the enemies with your gun. If you're playing with others, you get points by killing the enemy, and the person with the most points wins." The driver explains with his left hand on the wheel, motioning with his right, pretending to hold a gun.

The cab exits the freeway and approaches the entrance to Arlington.

"There they are," Bob says, his eyes staring ahead, endless rows of white-on-green stand on the grass that seem to go on forever.

The cab pulls up at the entrance, and the driver looks at the meter. "Thirty dollars," he says, turning to look at Bob. Bob pulls out some cash and hands it to him. As he does, the driver says, "Don't forget to check out the mall— lots of things to buy there."

Bob is looking at the crosses, his face sullen, lips tight. Then, motioning to the hill, he asks, "What would I buy to change this?"

The driver looks at him, puzzled, and does not reply.

Bob gets out of the cab and starts walking. His eyes stare ahead at the rows on the hill, row after row of white on the green grass. His thoughts are interrupted.

"Can I help you find a grave? Directions?" a ranger asks.

"No. I just wanted to see this place where you bury what you call warriors; I've heard it called the 'ultimate sacrifice,'" Bob motions at the crosses.

He walks up a path through the cemetery, away from the ranger. A woman comes up from behind him.

"How was the Acela?" she asks.

"It was fast by these standards. Good morning, Danielle."

Danielle looks perfectly a part of the somber scene in a stylish railroad hat with the brim pulled down low, a loose dark blue blouse, and jeans. She is slim and tall, with the same dark green eyes, light cinnamon skin, and white hair as Bob, though her walk is smoother.

They walk past the white crosses silently, slowing or stopping occasionally to read a name. Not a word is spoken. Finally, they reach the top of the hill. There, they both stop and look back down the slope.

"I thought this would remind us of what has happened and what we are trying to stop," Bob says.

"All these names, killed in wars. Not dying because of accidents, sickness, or aging. Wars, wars, wars," Danielle says in a whisper.

"Following orders," Bob says. He steps over out of the path and sits on the grass. Danielle joins him.

"How is your team, Danielle?"

"Anxious," she says. "We see the news, of course, and watch the behavior of those around us. We all have hope. We know what is possible."

"We know all the warheads of the United States submarine fleet are being changed, though we do not know to what or why. They will use Kings Bay submarine base to change them. Their huge dry dock would allow them to do it where satellites could not see them. Don is working with the team to get data," Bob says.

"Alongside our other methods, we have roses in the President's bedroom every night. We have a good chance with the First Couple; they have a good relationship. This would be a secret for the leader of the first world to share with his wife," Danielle says.

"What about the Pentagon?" Don asks, pointing in the distance.

"Difficult. Not impossible, but time-consuming. Still, our best chance is the First Lady and her husband. They have two children. My intuition says this mother wants to know why the warheads are being changed," Danielle says.

"I fear time is running out," Bob says. "I am being followed, as are others. We will hope your intuition is correct."

Danielle pulls out her phone, "Here is what happened last night." She pushes a button, and a recording begins to play.

"Craig, it's one a.m. Are you okay?" asks a woman's voice.

"Yes," says a deeper voice, presumably Craig.

Shoes slap against a wooden floor.

"God, I'm tired," says Craig.

The first voice, his wife, agrees, "You sound terrible."

"Hard meeting."

"Joint chiefs, right?"

"Yeah, all of them. All the military fuckers were there."

There's a brief pause before the wife asks, "What's wrong, Craig?"

"They're changing all our warheads."

"What...?"

"Carla, not tonight. I need some sleep. I'll talk to you about it tomorrow, but please, for tonight...just hold me."

"Come here," Carla answers, and sheets rustle as Craig climbs into bed.

Danielle pushes a button, and the recording stops. "That is what we have. My confidence is high. He will share this with her."

Bob and Danielle walk down the hill together in silence, reaching the cemetery entrance.

"Hungry?" Bob asks.

Danielle breaks into a smile. "Of course I am! What are you thinking?"

"IHOP," Bob says, also smiling.

She laughs, "Yes!"

"Good. I want to see something on our way. Only take a minute."

Bob hails a cab, and it pulls up to the curb.

"Where to?" the driver asks as they get in.

"Roaches Run Waterfowl Sanctuary."

"That's interesting. I've picked up plenty of fares here, and shopping or eating is usually the next stop," the driver responds as he pulls away.

"I needed something peaceful after all of those," Bob says, motioning to the hill.

The driver looks intently in the mirror at Bob and Danielle.

"I get it. My brother's up there. Iraq."

Bob leans forward in his seat. "I am sorry. You are the first person here that has talked about this. Thank you for your authenticity. So rare in this place."

"No problem. Like I said, I've picked up a lot of people here," the driver says, then asks, "Where are you from?"

"This is our first time here, but we have been to many places," Bob answers evasively. Danielle looks at him with just a slight smile.

The cab rolls on quietly for a while before the driver starts again. "After the towers went down, my brother and many others wanted to do something. He signed up and went looking for the weapons of mass destruction."

"How sad that must have been, thinking he was going to help. It is hardly a search for weapons of mass destruction when they are all around you," Bob sighs.

"You get it, man. I was angry for a long time. 'Following orders,' yeah, sure. Now I just see the stupidity," he pauses, calming himself, then switches topics. "I see you don't have a mask or breathing unit. Any reason? I don't mean to pry," The driver asks.

"Thank you for asking. No, we do not have either. Temporary solutions," Bob says.

"Like hunting for weapons of mass destruction when there are so many you can see them from space," Danielle says quietly.

The cab pulls up at the entrance to the Sanctuary. The driver turns to them and says, "Thirty-five dollars is your fare. I'm glad you got in my cab, and that's not just tip-talking. We're on the same page about many things."

Bob gets out a one-hundred-dollar bill and hands it to him. "Keep the change."

"Thank you for the generosity," the driver says, tipping his hat.

As they get out of the car, Bob replies, "If you wait here, I will give you another one of those. We won't be long," he says.

"You got it," the driver says and parks the car.

They walk through the trees by the water. A massive flock of red-winged blackbirds roosting, their singing signaling they would soon be flying.

A man sits on a stool by the water with a fishing pole.

"What kind of Pisces are in these waters?" Bob asks.

The man looks up at him, silent for a bit, studying Bob and Danielle, before answering, "Catfish, mostly. The occasional largemouth bass." He smiles. "I should be fishing for birds, or Avis, you'd call them."

Looking at the trees, Bob says, "I would guess a million or more red-winged blackbirds. I rarely meet someone who knows a species by its Latin name."

The man stands up. "My name's Matt, Matt Crawford. I study fish and birds. So yes, I am a fish and bird enthusiast."

"As are we, Matt," Bob extends his hand, "Bob Goeman. Matt, this is my associate, Danielle Webb." They shake hands before Bob continues, "Enthusiast is an interesting word to describe appreciation for living things. Flying and swimming, not walking like us. One breathes air, flying with feathers. The other breathes water, flying with fins. Most people here do not notice living things other than themselves."

"Except when they can use or eat it," Danielle says. The flock of birds departs, making their call out into the sky. She continues, "Their feathers create an airfoil. Amazing, they are so beautiful."

"There must be a million of them. Wow...Listen to them sing," Matt says as he watches them soar by.

"Yes. How do they do that?" Bob asks.

"They have a syrinx, similar to us, but..." Matt begins to answer until Bob interrupts him.

"No, I mean cooperation. Homo sapiens kill each other, seeking their place, their flight path. Those birds fly without fighting." Bob explains his question further.

"You know a lot about birds. When did you become so interested in them?"

"We just started looking at them," Bob says. Matt looks at him, a bit puzzled, but he simply says, "Enjoy your time here. We need to go."

The two of them slip into the cab. Bob hands the cabby another bill.

"Thanks for waiting," Bob says, "Keep that for the time. IHOP on 95. We love their maple syrup."

"How was the sanctuary?" the driver asks.

"So peaceful; we heard birds singing!" Danielle says with excitement. Again, the driver looks puzzled.

The cab leaves the curb and tries merging into the traffic but swerves violently as the driver swears. "Damn idiots, always trying to cut me off!"

"Yes, it seems to happen often here," Bob says as he looks out the window at one million red-winged blackbirds flying smoothly, effortlessly.

The cab rolls down 95. "So, are you a huge fan of IHOP?" The driver asks.

"We love their syrup," Bob repeats, then adds, "If you can wait again, that would be easy for us. Need to catch the Acela back to New York."

This time they drive on in silence. When the cab pulls up in front of the IHOP, Bob and Danielle get out, and Bob hands the driver another bill.

"Wait for us, and I will give you another."

"Thank you. This is my best fare of the day!"

"My pleasure. We will be back."

They walk into the restaurant, and the fragrance of eggs, pancakes, and sugar hits their nostrils. Both stand still for a moment, breathing deeply.

"It smells so wonderful," Danielle says.

"Yes. Yes, it does," Bob smiles.

They are sat in a booth, and the waitress comes over. "What can I get you two?"

"One waffle with strawberry syrup, please, and coffee," Danielle says.

"Me too. I have not tried the strawberry," Bob says.

The waitress writes down the order, and soon, the waffles come out with strawberry syrup. Bob and Danielle take turns pouring the syrup over their waffles, submerging them completely. She takes a bite first.

"Oh, *so* good."

She closes her eyes, chews slowly, and holds the food in her mouth to savor the flavor, and swallows. Her eyes open, and she smiles. They eat in silence, looking at each other, nodding their heads in deep appreciation. Bob finishes first.

"So, the devices are working okay? Are you sure you can retrieve their conversation again?" he asks.

"Yes. The future of so many may depend on a man telling his mate the truth."

"Truth. That is the only way to stop it," Bob says.

She sips the coffee, "The instant I have the recording, I will contact you."

"We better go so I can catch the train back," Bob says and sets some cash on the table. She nods at him with a bit of sadness in her eyes.

"Maybe…maybe we can convince them to not follow orders this time," Danielle says.

Bob nods. "It would be a first for them."

They get up and walk out of the diner to the cab.

"Train station," Bob says, and they pull away again

"What did you guys have?" The driver asks.

"A wonderful meal!" exclaims Danielle, and Bob agrees.

"Waffles with strawberry syrup! So good! The syrup just makes it amazing," Bob says.

"My best and most interesting fare of the day," the driver laughs, looking in the mirror, still just as puzzled.

— 11 —

Three Dreams

Grace looks at her dry erase board covered in equations. "Payload 119 kg" is written at the top of the board. She glances at the clock.

"Jack," she says, somewhat shocked, "I need to hurry."

She walks hurriedly from Parabola Systems to Jack's school, thinking deeply about her day. "Decrease payload," she mutters aloud and rubs her forehead in frustration.

Parents are leaving with their children when Grace arrives; laughter sprinkles the conversations. Children's and parents' faces smile as they meet, but in her mind, "decrease payload" interrupts her thoughts repeatedly. Twenty-six hundred warheads. Why? She hears her son's voice in her head, "Nine million people. So many people here."

A familiar voice interrupts her thoughts, "Grace De Falco! I'll tell them to bring Jack for you."

"Hi, Herschel," Grace sighs, "Sorry, I was thinking about work."

"Well, you can forget about that for now. Here comes Jack." Herschel laughs and points to Jack as he comes up the hallway. Lola is walking beside him, and they are both smiling and talking.

"Mom, my first day of summer school is over—my first day of summer school! I am so excited!" Jack exclaims.

"Would you like to introduce me to your friend?" Grace asks with a wave and looks at Lola, who smiles up at her. She also gives a little wave.

"This, this is Lola, Lola McGregor." Jack's smile is so vast, with some self-consciousness on his face and just a bit of a blush.

Grace looks at her while Herschel stands off to the side, soaking it all in. "Lola, I'm Grace, Jack's mother."

"Hi. Jack taught me a lot of history about where I live. He remembers so much!" Lola tells Grace; there is so much happiness in her voice.

"Lola helped me find my rooms," Jack explains, "I got lost once. Lola was there, though, and helped me," His right-hand flips slowly.

"I'm so glad you were here for Jack's first day." Grace smiles at Lola and Jack. Then she looks at Herschel, "I see what you mean about loving your job."

Grace and Jack walk away. Jack turns around to look at Lola, smiling and waving wildly. Turning back to Grace, he asks, "So, Mom, did you have fun at work today?"

"It's going to be a hard job," Grace says, "but I am so glad to have you here to make it easier." She looks at Jack, who looks up at her as they begin their walk to the Metro.

"Did you have a good day? You asked me a question about my day, so I should return the favor," Grace says, changing the subject.

"Mr. Jeff teaches many subjects," Jack replies. "This was our first day with him. We just talked. When we were talking, he asked a question I had never heard before." There's excitement in his voice. "He asked, 'Have you ever asked your parents, guardian, or any adult how their day was?' Then he said, please raise your hand if you can re-member and tell the class what they said."

"Wow, that's a great question!" Grace laughs.

Their conversation pauses as they reach a building undergoing renovation, and the sidewalk narrows due to scaffolding. Jackhammers rattle in the background.

"Did Mr. Jeff explain why he asked that question?" Grace asks.

"Yes," says Jack, "he did when no one raised their hand. He said we are now at the age where we are self-absorbed. We should become less and less as we grow. He said to ask other people questions. See what happens. Listen closely to people, see if they ask questions."

She puts her hand on his shoulder, and they walk in silence.

"You can't talk about your job in detail, can you?" Jack asks.

"My son, Mr. Perceptive, no, I cannot. This will be a difficult job for me."

They board the Metro and arrive at the apartment. Grace says, "Since it's our first day, I ordered a pizza; I will make a salad. How does that sound?"

"That's great! Can I call Dad and tell him about my first day?"

"Sure you can. You do that while I make the salad...or what we call salad now. I sure miss tomatoes, lettuce, spin-ach...." She sighs.

"The planet is changing. We must adapt. Most of our vegetables are now coming from South America or green-houses. We are starting a discussion group at school about how we can help. It will be interesting."

Jack gets on the phone. "Dad! My first day of school was today. A girl named Lola helped me. She was so nice to me. She smiled at me. I like her." Jack listens for some time. "The school is close. We ride the Metro and then walk.

It's easy. I think it will be a good summer, especially since
I have met a girl." The excitement in his voice is apparent
when he brings up Lola again. There is a pause, and a flustered Jack responds, "Yes, of course, she is pretty."

Grace can't help but smile when she hears Jack ask his
dad how his day was. She carefully continues to cut up the
arrangement of vegetables. Turnips, carrots, and cabbage.

"I'm glad you had a good class with your students,
Dad. Have a good night – oh, I hear the doorbell ringing. Our
pizza is here. Bye!" Jack hangs up the phone and follows his
mom to the front door, where she pays the pizza man.

The two of them sit down at the table and start eating, Jack wolfing down his food.

"Slow down, Jack! You act like you're starving."

"Okay, Mom," Jack replies, his mouth still full of pizza.
He swallows it quickly.

"Tell me about one of your classes," Grace says, taking
a bite of her salad.

Jack starts, "Well, after the Relax class, those of us
that were new went to a room where we were told about
some of the ways this school is different."

"Tell me about the Relax class."

"Well, the teacher said it was her favorite day, getting
to know everyone. She's nice. She asked everyone if they
would tell us who they were and something about ourselves. It was quiet at first. One boy scratched his arm a lot,
and another girl looked like she was trying to eat her pencil.
Another one was chewing on her hair. A boy never looked
up, another, and well, you know me, my knee felt like it
would come off my leg! I was so anxious.

"Ms. Alana, though, just kept being patient. She was
never tense like it was all okay. Like we were all okay if we
did not say anything. Finally, I said my name. Then she
said, 'Oh, thank you, Jack De Falco, for starting our day. You

made my heart happy. Who else is ready to tell Jack and me who you are?'"

"You were the first one to introduce yourself?" Grace asks with some amazement.

"Yeah, I was. Ms. Alana is genuinely nice. After each person, she said the same thing, 'You made my heart happy.' I think she likes her job," Jack finishes, taking another massive bite of pizza and chewing with his mouth open.

Grace gets up, goes to the sink, and refills her water glass so that Jack wouldn't see her holding back tears. She was so relieved and thankful. "Then what happened?"

"We all have teams when we have a new assignment in math or any subject. We all work together. They keep saying, 'teamwork.' I am excited."

"I'm glad you like it. I was worried, so I'm happy for both of us." Grace sighs. They finish supper, clean the table, and put the dishes in the dishwasher. "Jack, do you want to just walk up the block and back? It is so nice out."

"Sure, let's go."

They step out of the apartment and start down the street. "Mom, there are so many more people here compared to where Dad lives. There are only a few thousand in his town. So different. There are around nine million here. So many people. Do you think Lola likes me, or was it just because it was my first day?" Jack speaks quickly, changing topics at lightspeed.

Grace scrambles to keep up. "I've seen a lot of smiles in my lifetime. That smile on that girl's face was real."

"Mom, do you think she could be my girl-friend?" Jack asks.

Grace smiles. "Jack, you *just* had your first day of school. Slow down. She could be your friend first."

"Thanks, Mom. Imagine so many people here, and one of them smiled at me today. She is so pretty. One out of nine million smiled at me. I believe in science, but this was like, well, a miracle."

"Sometimes you amaze me," Grace says. She slows her walking and puts a hand on her son's shoulder.

They walk for a while in silence before turning around to go back to the apartment. Grace unlocks the door and says, "I'm going to get ready for bed. You should do the same."

. . .

The house is quiet, and the lights are off. Jack is asleep in a few moments, his eyelids racing with REM sleep. He is breathing easily, a slight smile on his lips. In his dream world, his hand wraps around Lola's. They're walking; he's gliding, his feet hardly touching the ground, floating. Lola's stride matches his in perfect rhythm, so graceful. She looks at him with complete admiration, her face glowing.

"Jack, you are so graceful. I feel like we are dancing," Lola says.

"Yes, I am graceful. Yes, we are dancing!" Jack yells and holds her hands tightly, never wanting to let go of this moment. His smile is as wide as his face, confident and radiant.

In the real world, Grace looks in at Jack, already asleep with his light still on by his bed. She walks over and turns it off, seeing his smile. Then, smiling in return, she walks down the hall to her bedroom, undresses, slips into bed, and is soon asleep.

Grace's head is soon tossing slightly back and forth on the pillow.

She is flying above the city, just over the tops of the skyscrapers, dressed in a black robe with her blond hair streaming behind her and the black robe making flapping noises. She sees people looking up as she descends toward them, getting closer, moving faster. The robe flaps louder and louder, her face stretched in the wind, the blond hair blowing straight back.

Millions of faces all looked at her. She falls faster, faster. The people on the ground scream as she falls towards them. The ground rushes to meet her. In the crowd is Jack's face, screaming at her, "Stop, mom! Mom! Stop it!"

• • •

Bob arrives back from Arlington late; it's midnight when he walks into his apartment. He finds himself going directly to bed. His eyelids flicker as he drops off to sleep.

In his mind, Jack, Grace, Sam, Billy, and the youth that tried to steal the purse look at an unending row of white tombstones that stretch to the sky. A flock of redwing blackbirds flies around the row of white tombstones. They all watch the flock, pointing.

"See, see how they fly? Over one million of them flying together, never colliding, all as one, singing the same song," Bob says, eyes following the birds that disappear over the horizon.

No Tip Today

Bob wakes to buzzing and ringing. He opens his eyes, blinking several times, and looks at his phone screen. "Don" scrolls across in bright letters.

He answers. "Hello, Don. Yes, I am awake…I was having this beautiful dream about a large flock of red-winged blackbirds I witnessed yesterday…Late getting back from my travels." Bob listens. "Let us talk about your concerns in person. Want some of Sam's coffee? Twenty minutes."

He hangs up and pulls on his jeans and sweatshirt. He brushes his teeth, grabs his bag, heads out the door, and stops in his doorway, immediately feeling the heat. He turns around and returns to change into a plain white shirt. After that, he is at Sam's in a few moments.

"Good morning, Bob! Usual coffee with four sugars?" Sam says.

"Yes, and the round food with holes – you call them donuts – one of those, please," Bob replies.

"Your first time having donuts? Special occasion?" Sam asks as he prepares the coffee.

"No, late getting back from Arlington last night."

"That's a long day. You took the Acela, I assume?"

"Yes, I did, Sam. Got back around eleven pm."

"Here you go. Man, it is *hot* this morning. When's it gonna cool off?" Sam puts the coffee and donut on the counter as he complains and begins to fan himself. "Each day, it seems harder to breathe, and I don't see how I can talk to customers with a mask on."

Bob bites into the donut , admiring the new flavor, and swallows, ignoring Sam's usual comments.

"This is exceptionally good, and it has sugar as an ingredient. How much today, Sam?" Bob asks and takes out his wallet.

"Ten dollars with the donut. They're two dollars each." Sam wipes the sweat from his brow with his handkerchief. "You never complain, Bob. My only customer who never complains."

"You mean about the temperature, the climate, the world? It is reality, Sam. This has been coming for a long time," Bob says.

Sam just looks at him.

Bob puts a ten on the counter. "Can I get another one of those donuts?"

"Never had a donut with sugar?" Sam chuckles to himself as he serves.

Bob takes another bite. "My friend is picking me up. Can you give me another cup of your excellent coffee, please?"

"Four sugars for your friend?" Sam asks as he fills another cup.

"Yes, please."

Sam hands over the cup. "Anyway, how was your trip to Arlington?"

Bob sighs, "I went to the National Cemetery where you bury your warriors. It is sometimes called the 'ultimate sacrifice.' All those graves, names, dates, all those people, gone. There in the distance, beyond the view of the white crosses, was the Pentagon, a war planning complex. A long day indeed."

Sam nods solemnly. "I came here from South America. Rich in resources, plundered by many. We have graves, too, most not marked. Ditches, gullies, rivers... I'm so thankful my family is here instead."

A horn honks, and Bob turns to see the white Toyota. "Glad you are here, Sam. Have a good day." Sam waves as he walks away.

He slides into the back seat and hands Don his coffee. "Appreciation for Sam's coffee. How was the trip?"

"I did make it to Arlington National Cemetery."

"What is it like?" Don asks.

"They made it look beautiful. Nothing like a battlefield. You can see their war planning complex from the cemetery, the Pentagon, and of course, you can see the White House," Bob says.

"What have our team members discovered at the White House?" Don asks.

"Danielle has confirmed the warheads are being changed. The President did not tell his wife what the new warheads were. He is concerned about it or would not have brought the subject up. She did not seem to be satisfied with his answer. They have two children. Danielle is confident that she will push him for an answer tonight."

Don stops at a light. "Let us go to the central location. We can discuss the various teams' input. I have something to show you that I think we will need."

They drive until they enter the Bronx in an industrial area. Don pulls up in front of a brick building at the end of an alley, pulls out his phone, and pushes some buttons. The garage door opens, he pulls in, and it closes behind them.

There is a small white delivery van with "David's Delivery Service" painted on it.

"We need a backup vehicle that has not been seen on cameras. When the mission is successfully completed, we will be able to leave undetected," Don explains to Bob, who nods his head in understanding.

"Optimism amidst this fear, this chaos. Don, you are an amazing team member."

"Thank you. I know there are no guarantees that the mission will work. It will take all of them," Don stops, looks down at the floor, "It would be the first time for them."

"Yes, Don, yes. I know. No guarantees, but worth the risk. I approve of the name of the van, by the way. We do have to slay Goliath."

"Yes, I thought it fit. David slaying the giant," Don says, nodding knowingly.

"Let us hope the myth becomes real."

Along one side of the warehouse is a small living room with a couch and a table with a TV, like a mechanic's garage. On the wall, there is a huge tv monitor. They walk over to the couch and sit down.

"When I reported our findings, I was reminded that we both speak many languages," Don says. "An operative for any country would have that same capability. The assumption that we found a Middle Eastern operation is not a fact. It could be any country. Many countries are dealing with crop shortages and starvation. It will get worse. Weather patterns are no longer predictable. A higher rate of crop failure is the result. As a result, you must plant more acres. How do you acquire more land for growing food?"

The two men sit in silence for a moment. Bob presses his lips together in a tight line, thinking of Don's question.

"Neither the United States nor any other country can use their traditional nuclear weapons without ruining the land they wish to occupy," Bob replies slowly. "Climate change has changed how you fight a war. The Americans must be changing their warheads to biological or chemical. You must be able to grow food after you have seized the land."

"So, you suggest these new warheads exist to kill people?" Don's voice is tense. "There is a treaty that outlaws these weapons!"

"Don. We know what happens with treaties here." Bob's voice is unusually sarcastic.

"Yes, you are correct. Sorry, I forget what we are dealing with."

They sit there in silence for a long time.

Finally, Don speaks. "You are suggesting that the weapons are only for killing people. Designed not to harm the air or water. Instead of destroying an entire city, kill the inhabitants. Move troops in to take over the functioning infrastructure. Eighty percent of the population lives in metropolitan areas. Agriculture production would be intact. Why destroy an entire city to kill eight million people? As terrible as it sounds, they are capable of it." Don looks at Bob.

Bob shakes his head, looking at the floor. "The warming climate and dropping oxygen levels have forced them to look at their weapons honestly. But, someone could think they could win with biological or chemical."

"Of course, it has to be a first-strike weapon," Don says. "Bob, we need proof for the mission to work. We need to find it quickly. This whole planet is on edge. It would not take much to push it to war."

Bob's phone rings and the screen lights up with the name Grace De Falco. He shows the screen to Don and excuses himself to take the call.

"Hello, Grace. Yes, I could make it by that time. I will see you and Jack then."

He finishes the call and turns to Don. "Jack and Grace wish to see me. I will walk with her from her employment to Jack's school. I will see if I can determine if she knows what is on the new warheads."

"Do you think that is why that man was following Grace? According to our data, she does computations for the weight of the missile's payload. She would not know what is on the missile," Don says.

"We assume but have no confirmation. If we are correct in our theory, others will look for answers everywhere. They may think Grace has an answer."

"So, what do you think we need to do now?" Don asks.

"Our answer could still come from the President's bedroom. Kings Bay Submarine base could be the other source."

"I agree. I will go to Kings Bay. Make sure we do all that is possible there. Take me to the airport," Don says.

Both get up and walk to the car.

"Do you think the Americans are preparing to launch a first strike with the Ohio submarines?" Don asks as Bob backs out of the garage and moves down the street.

"I don't know. I hope we get to use the van," Bob says quietly.

There is no conversation on the drive to the airport. When Bob pulls up in front of the airport unloading area, Don says, "In twenty-four hours, we will know."

They nod at each other.

In a taxicab behind them, a driver's sweaty face leans out the window and yells, "God damn you! Move!"

"Those could be the last words he says, or we hear," Don sighs as he exits the car.

The man in the cab behind them pulls up. "You're gonna make me late, and cost me a tip, asshole!" he shouts.

Bob rolls down his window. "Asking God to damn me? How does that work? Is there ever an answer?" Bob reaches into his pocket pulls out a one-hundred-dollar bill. The other driver looks at him strangely, then gets out and runs over and grabs the money.

— 13 —

A Very Strange World

"Mom, wake up! Wake up! You're having a nightmare!" Grace opens her eyes to find Jack looking down at her. "Are you okay? You were yelling something. I couldn't understand it."

Grace looks at him and runs her hand through her hair. "I'm okay. Nightmare. Wow. Have not had one for years. What time is it?"

"4:45 a.m."

She sighs. "Well, I might as well get up. The alarm will go off in thirty minutes. Sorry, Jack, I woke you up. You can go back to bed. I'm okay."

Grace rolls out of bed and slips on a robe. She makes her way to the kitchen and pushes the button on the coffee maker. Jack follows her and sits down at the kitchen table.

"What was your nightmare about, Mom? You were shaking when I woke you up."

Grace takes the coffee cup, dumps a bunch of sugar in, takes a sip, and joins Jack at the table.

"Well, without going into detail," she says, "it was an *unbelievably* bad dream. Very frightening...and sad."

"So what was it?" Jack presses, his voice is full of concern.

"This, I think, was about my job," Grace says reluctantly, taking another sip of her coffee. "What could go wrong. My concerns. So much of it is out of my control."

"You could quit your job, get another one? You're smart; you can do anything!" Jack suggests, his voice getting loud.

Grace just smiles. "Thank you for your concern, but no. I took this job, so I'll finish it. I really am fine, Jack. It's just a nightmare."

She downs the rest of her coffee. "I'm going to get my shower. A long one, I think. Are you going back to bed?"

"No, I think I'm going to work on my computer while you are in the shower."

Grace pats him on the shoulder, "Okay, brainiac. Don't work too hard." She walks to the bathroom and shuts the door.

Jack goes into his bedroom and turns on the computer. He searches "Parabola Systems," clicks on the Wikipedia page, and starts reading.

On the screen, he sees a picture of a submarine; under it is the caption, "Trident Missile Delivery System." He reads quickly; the pages roll by, and he keeps changing the screens. He does not hear the shower turn off or the door to his room open.

"What are you reading?" Grace says as she walks over to his desk and sees the pictures of a Trident Missile in flight.

"I knew when you were helping on the Starlink Project for Elon Musk, launching multiple satellites into space. Well, you know me; after your nightmare, I thought I would do a little research on Parabola Systems. The Ohio class submarine fleet carries 2,600 warheads. A multiple launch scenario. Obviously not communication satellites."

His voice rises in volume again. He turns from the computer and looks at his mother, his radiant smile gone and his hand flipping rapidly.

Grace's face is proud and sad at the same time as she considers the brilliance and intuition of her son, and his caring for her. "Jack…" She stops and tries again. "Jack, I don't like the way the world is. We just hope no one tries anything. We hope what we do here stops them from trying anything."

Jack turns off the monitor on the computer. "Me too, Mom, me too. I hope what you're doing helps. I am sad because it causes you nightmares and we have these weapons. 2600 hundred warheads on just the submarines! That's not counting any of the others. That's just the United States. Humans are stupid!"

"You're right," Grace agrees, "but the reality is that we must have weapons to protect ourselves."

"Nuclear weapons would ruin the environment! It is stupid to even have them!" Jack's voice gets louder and louder.

"Other countries, some that don't like us at all, they have nuclear weapons, too. We would be powerless without them. That is the world we live in. That is reality," Grace says, trying to stay calm. She pats him on the shoulder, but he shrugs her off.

"The world is stupid. You can't deny that!"

"Yes, it is stupid, but *it is the world we live in*. We can't change this," Graces says, almost pleading.

Jack storms out of his room and goes into the bathroom. Soon Grace hears the shower running. She lingers for a moment, then enters the kitchen and takes out a bowl and pancake mix.

A little while later, Jack emerges from the shower, drying his hair.

"I made some pancakes," Grace offers quietly.

"Thanks, Mom..." His voice is quieter now. "About earlier...I just don't get it, the nuclear weapons. I never have, and I don't think I ever will." He seems to be fighting to keep his voice calm.

"It's okay. I understand," Grace says quickly, relieved that he's willing to talk. "It worries me too. That's why I had the nightmare. For now, though, please... let's just have breakfast, okay?"

Soon they're sitting at the table, and Jack is wolfing down pancakes; some syrup sticks to the corner of his mouth, and his smile is back.

"Thanks," he says at last. "It's been a long time since we had pancakes." After a brief pause, he says, "I had a dream about Lola. We were dancing." His eyes shine as he takes another bite. "We were holding hands. Really, we were just walking and then dancing! I was so graceful in my dream, and Lola told me I was a good dancer. There was music, and we danced!"

Grace smiles at her son. "Now, *that* is a good dream to have. So, ready for another day at school?"

"Yes. I'm hoping I get to see Lola again." But then his smile falters. "I have a pimple on my face. It looks gross."

Grace waves a hand. "You're so handsome, and besides, all the other boys your age have pimples, too. They'll go away."

"But I want to look good."

"Your concern about looks has something to do with this, Lola," Grace says with a sly grin, but it softens immediately. "I love that you're honest about your feelings about your looks. I was never able to do that as a child. Good for you. But it really is just a bump on your face. It'll be okay. I'm sure Lola won't mind."

Jack blushes but still looks downcast. "But she's so pretty..."

Grace sees her opening and asks, "Yes, Jack, she is. Would she still be pretty if she had a pimple or a zit?"

Jack blinks, surprised, then smiles. "Yes, she would."

"Okay, genius, why would she still be pretty?"

"She was so nice to me."

Grace lightly claps her son on the back. "And there you go! Now, finish your cereal. Let's get ready to catch the Metro."

Grace heads to her bedroom and lays out a blouse and slacks on the bed. She removes her bathrobe and briefly stands in front of the mirror. She studies her body, knows her breast are starting to sag, and remembers Bob handing the purse to her.

"*I apologize for my locker room talk. Beauty is on the inside.*"

He wasn't looking at my body, she thinks; he *was looking into me. Who is he?*

After dressing, she stands in front of the mirror and starts applying her makeup. She's detailed in the process, painstakingly using each product and studying its effect on her face.

Ten minutes later, Jack yells, "Hurry up! You take too long with your makeup."

She smiles at last. With one more lipstick application and a final look in the mirror, she turns to go.

Jack is waiting for her at the front door. "Hurry *up*, Mom! I don't want to be late." He looks at her, then in the mirror, then back at her with disapproval.

"I'm coming Jack, I'm hurrying," Grace says.

"You really are pretty," Jacks says, looking at her intently.

Grace doesn't reply. Instead, she says, "I'm ready, so let's go."

"Do we have time for a donut?"

"Yes, I think we do. I could use a cup of coffee too."
They walk quickly to Sam's.

Sam greets them cheerily. "Hello, Grace! Good
morning, Jack!"

"Hi, Sam! Just a donut for me, please," Jack says.

Grace puts money on the counter, "Coffee with the
usual sugar, thank you, Sam." As he works, she adds, "Oh, I
forgot! Give me another coffee, please, just like mine."

With coffee and donut in hand, they turn to catch
the Metro. On the platform, Grace sees Billy standing off
by the wall by himself, and they head over. Grace hands
him the coffee.

"Grace, God's favor," Billy says as he accepts the cup.
"Thank you. And who is this young man with you today?"

"Billy, this is my son, Jack. Jack, this is Billy."

"Jack was originally John, meaning God's Graciousness," Billy says, nodding.

"You are correct," Jack agrees, "I have researched my
name. But what is the meaning of 'Billy?'"

"Determined protector," Billy says proudly, taking his
Bible from his pocket. "With God's help, of course."

"I hear the train coming. Billy, we'll talk more tomorrow, but it was good to see you again."

"God and I will be here. We look forward to it."

Jack waves at Billy. "I have a religion class today. I'll
have questions for you tomorrow!" Billy waves in return.

With that, they hurry to the boarding platform.

"So, what's wrong with Billy? Why did you give
him coffee?"

Grace shakes her head. "The morning I almost had
my purse stolen, I saw Billy. The young man who tried to
steal from me could have gotten money by asking, and Billy,
of course, is homeless. I felt blessed that morning, I decided
to pass that on and give him a twenty-dollar bill."

Jack tilts his head. "Are you saying we should give people money if they don't have any?"

Grace chuckles, "Oh, Jack, you ask such great questions. Enough about that, though. Tell me what's going on at school today."

"Well, I'm not sure; it's just the second day. World Religions is the class that I am most intrigued about today. We start with Islam. I hope I get to ask questions!"

"So do I!" Grace beams. "So do I. Remember what Bob said. 'People will learn when we ask questions.'"

"Yes, he did! I can hardly wait," Jack says excitedly.

The conductor announces, "White Plains." They stand up, reach the door, and disembark the train.

"What if we call Bob?" asks Jack," I would like to tell him about my school."

"Let me think about it. He was interesting."

They exit the train and walk to the school. Grace has her hand on Jack's back for a bit.

"I am so glad your first day went so well," she says, "there are people at your school who love their job."

Jack smiles his big smile, and they walk together. He is quieter than usual, walking on his toes and flipping his hand more quickly than average.

"Jack, you seem a little quiet," Grace says.

"It's just…you want to help a homeless person, yet work on a weapons system that can deliver 2,600 nuclear warheads." He stops and looks at her, the smile dropping as he says, "This is a very strange world."

Grace just looks at her eleven year old son. She reaches up and puts her hand on his shoulder, and gives it a pat, trying to keep her face void of expression. "Yes, yes it is," she replies softly.

They lapse into silence for the rest of the walk.

A man neither of them sees watches them go, and reaches up to his chest, adjusting the very slight bulge under his jacket.

— 14 —

Always and Forever

Grace and Jack walk up to the school to find Herschel standing outside. "Good morning, Grace and Jack. Did you tell your mother about your first day?" Herschel asked.

"Yes," Jack replies.

"Hi, Jack," a small voice calls from behind him. Jack whips around to see Lola standing behind him.

"L-Lola! Hi! Are you...are you here to...to walk me to class?" he stammers, looking down at his feet.

"No, silly," Lola giggles, "You know where it is!" She sways slightly back and forth. Jack's blush bursts across his face; he's so flustered that it takes him a moment to realize he has dropped his folder, scattering papers on the floor.

"I am so clumsy! So uncoordinated! What is wrong with me?" He gets down on his knees to pick them up and finds Lola doing the same.

"They're just papers, not eggs," Lola reassures him as she straightens the pages out for him.

"Sometimes I wish I was somebody else!" Jack shouts with a cracking voice. As he straightens up, he looks at Lola and realizes she's already looking directly at him.

"Jack…let me tell you a secret? I want to be different, too. I wish I were smarter! I work so hard to get a passing grade. Why do you think I'm in summer school?" She hands the papers to him as he breathes heavily, chest heaving up and down as he tries to calm down.

"Maybe I could help you study sometime?" Jack mumbles, and she smiles.

"I could use that. When we take a break from studying, we can play catch with eggs!"

Jack looks at her. *She was here yesterday to greet me on my first day. She was told to do that. No one told her to be here today. She wanted to be here. To see me.* In that instant of joy, he finds his voice, and it fills the hall.

"Lola…thank you for being here this morning." He grins. "Playing catch with eggs! I would need a net!" They both laugh. With the papers picked up, they walk down the hall; Jack doesn't even hear his mother saying, "Have a good day!"

"So, what subject do you have trouble with?" Jack asks as they walk.

Lola groans. "All of them, Jack, all of them!"

"Good. It will not make any difference which subject we start with!" Jack says with a smile.

Lola laughs, "No, I guess it won't."

The two walk, disappearing down the hall, from Grace and Herschel's view.

"There they go," Herschel chuckles, smiling after them.

"You know, Herschel, I think you're right. Jack has a friend!" Grace smiles and feels herself relax slightly. Jack felt safe here, and had a friend who accepted him for who he was; it was more than she'd hoped for in two short days. "You're right; this is an amazing place." With that, she smiles at the security officer. "Have a good day." He waves her off, and she makes her way to work.

When she gets to the Parabola Systems building, she's surprised to see Wayne's friendly face by security.

"Good morning, Grace! How was Jack's first day?" Wayne asks.

"His first day was perfect! I can't imagine a better school for him," she replies as she sets her phone on the counter.

"Glad that he's enjoying it. That school is a great asset to us. So many of our employees send their kids there," Wayne says, then shifts gears. "I wanted to go through security with you this morning. If you have any questions, I can answer them."

"Okay, why don't you walk me through it?"

He comes to stand beside her and preps as he talks. "This is like the airport, but it is recorded. Your body shape, what you're wearing, what you carry, that kind of thing. Security here treats everyone as a spy."

Wayne removes his shoes and puts them on the belt that goes through the scanner, puts his St Christopher medal and places it in a container, then walks forward and stands in the enclosure. The device circles him three times. "It's storing data," he explains, speaking loudly over the machine. "Comparing each day, looking for differences using algorithms. Much higher tech than the airport, though. It can get irritating, but it's necessary."

"I understand," says Grace, "So, this happens every day?"

"Yep, every day when you arrive and when you leave. There are no secrets here."

Grace takes off her shoes, puts her bag on the belt, and takes her turn in the enclosure while Wayne puts his boots on and watches her.

"We had an incident a little while back. Someone planted a recording device in a person's coat. We never discovered who, or how, or what they were looking for," Wayne explains. Grace's eyes watch the machine circle around her; she listens to it hum. "Security here never stops. The background checks and the vetting of potential employees are, of course, very thorough, but that continues even after you're hired. Grace if you put extra money into any account your name is on, or even remotely connected to, security will know it. The company now monitors your financial life and your contacts."

"I remember the document I signed," Grace nods. "Parabola Systems has permission to access 'any of my communication and financial records at any time.' I've no secrets to keep." She exits the machine and continues, "All the world's powers, though, have their secrets. Countries want to know each other's secrets. Everyone tries to keep their secrets secret."

"You've nailed it," Wayne says, "We're a world of secrets."

"It does make you wonder what would happen if there were no secrets," Grace says. She chuckles.

"What's so funny?"

"Oh, nothing. It is just something Jack would say. 'No secrets.' Or maybe something the man on the train might say."

"Oh! I got that report you asked for, on your friend on the train. He is a photographer and only recently has a presence in the USA. Speaks multiple languages. He did some work for National Geographic on the Ukrainian genocide."

"Thank you," Grace says, "Jack and I were talking about him just this morning. We enjoyed him. He is just so…different; he listens so well. I've never met anybody like him." She thinks back to her son's face when Bob entertained his questions.

"Friendships are hard to establish in the city. I hope it works for you. We all need friends," Wayne replies.

They stand silently for a moment; Finally, she says, "Thank you again, Wayne. I appreciate it. Do you have a moment? I need to talk to someone about my duties here."

"Now works for me. We can talk in your office," Wayne says as they exit the elevator. Grace swipes her card in the door, and they enter her office. She puts her things on the desk, leans back, and rests, folding her arms across her chest. She lets out a deep sigh.

"I had a nightmare last night," she confides after a few moments of internal debate. "Dressed in an all-black robe, falling through the sky towards people. They were screaming. I'm...kind of embarrassed to bring this up on my second day. I just...I felt like I could talk to you."

He nods. "You're not the first to come to me with something like this. Thank you for your trust. Especially now, with the way things are, I have this conversation often with employees. I also have the occasional nightmare. We work for the military-industrial complex. I don't know why we're changing payloads; we just follow the orders. We don't get to know when, why, or what." He pauses. "The crop shortages around the world, weather patterns changing, the oxygen level dropping. It has put us all on more of an edge.'

"Jack asked me what I did here. When I told him I was working on an important project, he said, 'You are working on a weapon system.'"

"It sounds like Jack reads his mother well." Wayne sighs. "We hope it helps keep the world safe by showing force. Until humankind changes, I'm afraid that's what we must do."

"Yeah, you're right, of course. To think otherwise is childish," Grace sighs.

"Not childish," he corrects, "hopeful. We must hope, Grace. It keeps us sane. Don't worry about talking about your fears. That's part of my job." He reaches up and touches the St. Christopher medal.

"Thank you so much for listening to me. I hope I didn't…well, like I said, it's embarrassing to bring up."

Wayne smiles. "Forget it. How about you and I have lunch in the cafeteria? I'd love to hear more about your son. He sounds like an interesting person. Noon?"

Grace nods with a smile. As he leaves, she pulls a business card from her purse and dials the number, but the call is routed to voice mail.

"Bob, this is Grace De Falco. Jack and I would enjoy seeing you again. We get on the Metro around four thirty every day, so we get to the station around four. Give me a call, and we can ride the train together again. Jack will have lots of questions, I'm sure. Thanks, bye."

After hanging up, she goes to the dry erase board. "Decrease payload," she says—her face scrunching.

The morning passes quickly. Occasionally, Grace talks to herself aloud.

"Maintain altitude for four-hundred kilometers? Strange reentry…a glide path?"

Eventually, she looks up at the clock and sees it's nearly noon. She arrives at the cafeteria to find Wayne waiting for her.

"Grace! I think you'll find that the food here is excellent. Grab a tray."

They go down through the line. Grace stops and looks down at the food. "Lettuce? Real lettuce?" she mumbles aloud, then notes joyfully, "Even tomatoes!"

Wayne hears her and smiles.

They find a table next to the windows where they can see the city below them.

"This is a great view," Grace comments, then gestures to her plate. "I took a lot of lettuce for my salad *and* a tomato. A tomato! I hope that's ok. It's the first lettuce I've seen in a long time. Who's your supplier?"

"We have a small garden on the roof. Several of the employees take care of it. It's a great diversion from what we do here," Wayne says somberly.

"A garden...yes, that would be a pleasant diversion."

"Enjoy your salad, Grace. Tell me about Jack."

She puts salad dressing on her salad as she is talking. "He is brilliant, if a bit different. Remembers most of what he reads and has such a bright mind." She spears a cherry tomato, takes a bite, chews, and swallows, savoring the experience before she continues, "He asks great questions, things I'm just asking myself as an adult. At the same time, he's just starting puberty. He's so honest about...well, his developing body. It's a little funny and a little spooky. You have children, Wayne?"

"Yes, grown and married now. Two grandchildren, though, and one has some different things about him, too. Only three years old, but you can tell. It's fascinating to see them grow and change." He laughs. "Tell me about Jack's first day at school."

"Lola is the girl's name that greeted him yesterday morning, apparently. Jack couldn't find one of his classes, so she helped him. And a teacher, when they all must introduce themselves, helped ease the tension. Jack spoke first! I couldn't believe it. First!" Grace shakes her head. "And when I went to get him yesterday, Lola walked with him to the pickup point. His talking about his first day at school brought me to tears; I had to get up and refill my water glass so he wouldn't see."

Wayne laughs again. "Oh, I love to hear stories like this from our people!" His boisterous conversation has people turning and smiling. Clearly, they've heard this before. Grace sees he has a connection with his employees. .

There's a buzz from Wayne's pocket. "Ah, excuse me." He pulls out his phone, listens, and then says, "You have a call. They always let me know in case someone's not in their office. Apparently, it's Bob Goeman? That was the photographer, right?"

"Yes, I left him a message," she smiles. "I should head back to answer him."

"No, don't worry about it. Here you go," Wayne says. He takes his phone and pushes a button, handing it to her. She takes it gratefully.

"Yes, this is Grace... Hi, Bob, yes, we'll be at the train station in White Plains around four. We leave for the station at 3:40... Oh, in the morning? We'll be at the station at seven a.m." She listens. "That would be great! We'll look forward to seeing you today, then. Thanks. Bye."

She hands the phone back to Wayne. "Thanks."

"How did you meet this, Bob Goeman?" Wayne asks.

"I was on my way to the Metro, and, I screamed at a rat. Bob was taking pictures of it, calling it by its Latin name. He has this accent I can't pinpoint." Grace explains everything from the beginning, returning to how Bob immersed himself in the environment and everything in the moment. She explains the attempted purse snatching and how he was so calm compared to everyone around him. Wayne leans on folded hands, listening to Grace finish her story. "He looked at me in a way I have never experienced. He wasn't looking at me like some men do, but almost like... like he was looking *into* me. I felt so calm with him around."

"Calmness in all of this. I could use that. Your son obviously feels this man's calmness, too. I'd love to meet him," Wayne says, then looks at his watch and gets up, "Well, I should be going. I hope we can do this again, and I hope your meeting with this man goes well. Call me if you need anything." Wayne exits the cafeteria, stopping by to say hello to several people on his way out. Grace watches him as he goes; he smiles and touches people on their shoulders. He talks to his people with the same kindness he showed her.

Grace finishes her lunch and returns to her office. At 3:25, she steps back from the dry erase board, grabs her purse and phone, heads down the elevator, and goes through the security scan again. She exits the building and walks onto the busy sidewalk.

There, she sees Bob standing at the curb, minding his own business and looking up at the sky to watch a flock of pigeons. As she moves closer he begins studying the traffic, his head turning left to the right to watch a taxi cut off another, and listening to horns and brakes screeching in the never-ending din.

She walks up behind him. His face is straight ahead, but somehow, he knows she's there.

"Hello, Grace De Falco. I remember Jack saying you worked at Parabola Systems. I thought we could walk from here. I had a stressful drive from the airport," Bob says without turning around.

She pauses a moment, puzzled. "Yes, that'd be fine. It's only five, maybe ten minutes from here." She pushes the crosswalk button, and Bob starts to step out just as the light changes, so she quickly puts her hand on his shoulder. "Whoa, stop! You've got to wait a few seconds and look up the street for oncoming traffic."

"Thank you," Bob says, his voice still calm and even. "I forgot that instructions here are not always followed."

"Yeah, that's why you hear the horns, the cursing, and the brakes. This city is nothing but chaos! You could get hurt doing that," she scolds.

"Thank you again, Grace De Falco." They cross the street together and start their walk.

"So, did you get any good pictures today?" she asks.

"No, I did not work on any photography today. Working on other things. How was your work today?"

"Had an excellent talk with the man who hired me. He's a good listener. Concerned for his people, want to know that they're cared for and happy," Grace explains.

"Being concerned for others, wishing for their happiness. These are good traits for a human being, I believe."

"Yeah, I think so. Did you make it to Arlington?"

"Yes, I did."

"How was that?"

"Sad, but we can save that visit for another time. Please tell me about Jack's first day. I know you were concerned about how it would go for him."

"Oh, Jack's first day was amazing. He has a great teacher. She sees all of the kids as people who could help the world. And there were students to welcome new people to school, and a girl named Lola welcomed Jack. She was wonderful and helped Jack so much by just being friendly!" Grace the says softly, "The whole place…well, it makes me feel hopeful. Those people love what they do."

"Grace, do you love your job? Does your job make you feel hopeful?"

They walk some distance before she speaks. "I…can't talk in detail about my work, but…I love problem-solving and math. I just wish I knew what my work was being used for. It's worrisome to not know."

"Parabola Systems, I know, is one of many enterprises that design and manufacture military equipment. A mother, I am sure, would have conflicts about that. It sounds like you are working on something, and you do not know what."

"When I interviewed for the position, I was asked if this would bother me. I said no. The entire world is armed. I know we have to defend ourselves." She sighs, "I took the job because of the money. Justifying I needed the money for Jack's education. So the answer to your question is yes and no. Yes, I know what I'm working on, but no, I don't know why. I don't think I can change this world."

"The person making screws that hold a panel in place on a missile, a menial job, says the same thing. If you quit, they will find someone else to do your computations. That coupled with the world changing rapidly now. Millions are facing the dilemma of food, shelter, and, yes, even air to breathe. None of you think you can change this world."

"I just want Jack to be okay," Grace replies tightly. Her brows furrow together at the thought of anything happening to her son.

"I understand, Grace. You are a mother."

"So your photography. How do you see that in this conversation?"

"My work does not change the world unless the images are acted on by others."

"Like your set of pictures in publications on Ukraine?"

"Yes, only if people act on what they see."

They reach a crosswalk and wait beside a building under renovation. Several construction workers position barricades a few feet out from the side of the building and bolts them together.

Bob and Grace start to move cautiously around, but the construction worker shouts, "You're okay! Go right ahead. You're not in our way. They're just getting this ready. We're putting some new siding on the building. City code."

Bob and Grace wave in thanks and keep moving. They reach the crosswalk on the other side of the school, and Grace pushes the button. Bob waits this time until she starts.

They walk up to the school entrance, and, as before, Herschel's voice booms out from behind the glass. "Good afternoon, Grace De Falco!"

"Hello again, Herschel!" Grace gestures to Bob. "This is a friend of ours, Bob Goeman." To Bob, she adds, "Herschel is school security as well as public relations."

Herschel waves. "Welcome, Bob Goeman."

"Thank you for the friendly greeting, Herschel," says Bob, "You seem incredibly happy here. Grace was telling me this was a very hopeful place."

"Yes, it is. I love this job. You nailed it; it gives me hope."

"What did you do before you had this job?"

Herschel pauses, blinking. "Mr. Goeman asks good questions. I was a prison guard, but I wanted to do that job differently than the job description."

"Ah," Bob says, looking him over. "And now you have your perfect job."

"Yes, I do; yes, I do. Speaking of, I take security very seriously. You're approaching our safe zone, Mr. Goeman. Would you be kind enough to provide me a photo ID so you can be in our system as a safe visitor?"

Bob smiles. "My pleasure." He puts his ID in the drawer.

Herschel takes it, scans it in, and puts it back. "Here you go," he says as the drawer opens. "This way, the computer won't alert me with a 'stranger' notification when you approach the building. The AI didn't recognize you, so I got an alert on the screen."

Bob nods approval.

Just then, Jack and Lola appear.

"Hi, Mom," says Jack, then he grins. "You brought Bob! Bob, this is my friend Lola Mc Gregor." Jack's smile is big, and Lola's eyes are wide; the energy coming from both is electric. Bob waves to Lola, and she waves shyly back.

Reluctantly, they separate as Jack steps toward his mother. "See you tomorrow, Lola," Jack says.

Grace, Jack, and Bob walk to the crosswalk. Jack turns once to see if Lola has left.

"So, how was school?" asks Grace as the three of them cross the street.

Jack starts talking rapidly. "The class on world religions began today. Our instructor is Mr. Jeff. He began by having us introduce ourselves, then he talked a little about himself and how his parents and grandparents were Methodists. His wife's exposure to religion was Catholic, though. Mr. Jeff told us to become comfortable talking about our faiths. Telling us the community you were born into largely determines what faith you will follow."

"My mother and father were both Methodists," Grace chimes in. "Your father is Catholic. His father, mother, grandparents, and great-grandparents can trace their history back to a little village in Italy; they're all Catholics."

"Yes, that is what Mr. Jeff was trying to get us to look at. Most of the world's population didn't choose their faith. It's just the faith they were taught," Jack says.

"Jack, did you ask any questions today?" Bob asks.

"Yes, I did. I asked why we were studying religion. It doesn't seem to be a particularly useful subject."

"What was Mr. Jeff's reply?"

"He said by knowing something about the world's religions, we can realize that there is something in each religion that's good for humanity. You can get perspective by listening to other people who have a faith that is different from yours. He said, 'Mr. De Falco, did I answer your question?' That's how he talks to us—like we're adults!" Jack laughs. "I liked it when he called me 'Mr. De Falco.' It made me feel grown up." In a lightning-fast topic change, Jack asks, "Mom, Bob, do you think I should kiss Lola?"

"Jack!" Grace splutters, "No, you've only known her for two days! What are you thinking?"

Jack deflates slightly. "I was trying to be honest with you about my feelings. Maybe I should call Dad tonight. I'm...well, I have feelings."

"Well, we certainly got away from the subject of religion in a hurry," Bob turns to look at them both, chuckling a little bit.

"Do you have a wife or a girlfriend?" Jack blurts.

"No, Jack, I do not. I am rarely in the same spot long enough, and right now, I cannot see that being an option for me. You, however, will be driven to act. You could consider holding her hand first."

The sounds of the traffic surround them as they come to another crosswalk.

"Bob, what religion are you?" Jack asks.

"A good question to ask if you want to know someone. Their answer is what you need to be ready for. Being ready is more important than the question."

"What do you mean, ready?" Jack tilts his head, frowning.

"Not judging. Judging others has led to heartache, violence, and war."

"Well, I think I'm ready. What religion are you?" Jack pushes.

"I cannot define Jack De Falco, his mother Grace, nor God. You and all of this are a miracle. So, I worship this. A great question, Jack. You will find most people here do not answer that question truthfully. Many of them have doubts about their religion, faith, a creator. They fear sharing it because they believe people will judge them."

Jack looks at Bob, saying nothing but contemplating this response.

Grace watches and listens without interrupting until they are finished, then adds, "Thank you, Bob, for listening to Jack's questions."

Bob merely nods and smiles.

Jack is ahead of them as they reach the entrance to the train station. He waits by the stairs for Grace and Bob to catch up to ensure he doesn't lose them in the mass of commuters making their way home. Turning, he sees Billy standing off to the side.

"Mom, there's Billy!"

She nods, and they make their way over to him.

"Ah, "God's Favor, God's Graciousness, and the man whose breath will not be a passing shadow," Billy says with a wave. "How was your religion class today, Jack?"

"Excellent. I've decided to study before I choose what religion I follow."

"That seems wise to me. What else did you discern from class?" Billy asks.

"We need to tell each other what we believe. Try to remember our beliefs may not be facts."

"Insightful. 'You will know each other, and it will set you all free.' John 8:33," paraphrases Billy, pulling his small pocket Bible out. Jack studies him closely.

"Do you have a question for me?" Billy asks.

"Hope we get to see you tomorrow. We'll be at Sam's coffee in the morning," Jack replies simply.

The train's noise gets louder as it approaches. As they turn to go to the boarding platform, Bob glances to his left and sees, several yards away, the man who was following Grace. His eyes focused intently on Bob.

The train arrives, and the doors open, ushering the three into the car together. They take a seat, and Bob looks out the window to find the man's eyes looking at him as the train pulls away.

The three of them settle down in their seats as the train moves ahead: Jack in the middle, Bob next to the window, and Grace next to the aisle.

"Jack, you looked as if you were going to ask Billy a question. I am curious what you thought about asking him and why you stopped," Bob comments.

"I wanted to ask him why he is homeless," Jack says. "then I stopped and thought that would be rude. He seems genuinely nice; he's intelligent, articulate, and well-read. It just seems strange that he would be homeless."

"Good for you. You thought twice before asking a question that would have, been uncomfortable for the man. I do not know why Billy is homeless," Bob says.

"Bob, where's home for you?" Grace asks.

He is quiet as he ponders her question, "For now, here. I travel light, so home is pretty much wherever I am."

"White Plains, next stop," the intercom calls as the train rolls into the station.

"How far do you live from the station?" Grace asks, trying again.

"Only about ten minutes north. About five minutes from Sam's," he says.

"We're south, about the same time. We're practically neighbors," Grace says with a smile. They exit the train and go up the stairs to the streets above as she continues, "I found a sandwich shop just up the street when I came here for my interview. May Jack and I buy you a sandwich?"

"That would be nice," Bob smiles.

"I'm pleased, Mom. I never knew I could be so happy. This must be love," Jack rambles, his voice filling with excitement before he stops and thinks to himself. "Mom, can I call Dad tonight and talk to him about Lola?"

"You can call your dad anytime you want to. You don't have to ask." Grace explains. They walk up to a café door of Vitro's Deli, as she says, "The sandwich I had was excellent. Do you know what you might want, Bob?"

"No, I will just take your lead. Whatever you get, make mine the same."

"Okay. Jack, you want roast beef and mayo?"

Jack nods.

"Okay, I'll get it. Can you two get us a table?" Grace asks.

Bob and Jack go outside and pick a table facing the street. As they sit, Bob turns to Jack. "What does your father do? John, I believe, is his name?"

"Yeah, that's it. Dad teaches world religion at the University of Bingham. He recently took a position there. It's about three hours from here."

"Do you like the school there?"

"I don't know yet. We just recently moved there. I'll find out this fall. School starts there in late August." After a brief pause, he asks, "What's the difference between love and infatuation?"

"Jack, you are infatuated with Lola. That is a good thing! A wonderful thing. But you will find out if there is something more with time."

Grace walks up to the table with a tray, playing it up as she serves. "Here you go, men. Supper is cooked." She sets the tray on the table with the sandwiches and three paper cups.

A skinny Chinese boy comes over to fill the cups with water. When Bob thanks him in Mandarin, the boy looks surprised and thrilled. They have a short conversation before the boy gives Bob a slight bow, turns, and walks away.

"You speak Mandarin!" Jack exclaims.

"Yes, one of many languages. Somehow, you have thousands of them," Bob answers.

Grace raises an eyebrow at Bob. "How many languages *do* you speak?"

"Several," he says as he takes a bite from his sandwich.

Jack eats as he has never eaten before. Bob studies him, watching him enjoy the food with a smile.

"Jack's a growing boy. You seem amazed to see him eat," Grace says as she sees Bob smiling at Jack.

Bob chuckles to himself before he takes another bite from his sandwich. As he does, Grace notices a bracelet on his wrist. It's about an inch wide and gray, with different symbols. It fits tightly with no visible clasp or latch.

"Your bracelet is so interesting," she says.

Bob glances at his arm. "Thank you. It is a gift I have had for a long time." He changes the subject. "It is amazing to watch the human body change, grow, mature. Jack has a great zest for life."

"Tomorrow, I am going to kiss Lola!" Jack blurts suddenly, derailing the current conversation. Bob laughs at his eagerness.

"Jack, patience!" Grace says and blushes deeply.

"Oh, and Mom, I almost forgot to tell you. There's dinner for parents and friends tomorrow at the school. Sorry, I was supposed to bring a slip home."

"That sounds like fun. What are we eating?" she asks.

"It's a secret." Jack grins.

"Well, I look forward to it. Can you invite anyone?"

"Yes, I can. Bob, would you join us? Lola and I are working together on food." Jack's eyes are bright and wide.

"I will be there," Bob agrees.

The adults finish their sandwiches first and sit silently in each other's company for a little while. Grace and Bob are watching Jack devour the roast beef. After the meal, the young boy cleans the table quickly.

Bob pulls a bill out of his billfold; Grace glances and sees the one-hundred-dollar bill. "Oh, Bob, I have some change. I can get the tip," she says, but Bob walks over to the boy and hands him the bill anyway.

The boy bows, offering words in Mandarin before taking off.

Bob comes back over to the table. "Obviously here illegally, been here a couple of weeks, twelve in the family. I watched Jack eat and talk about kissing a girl for the first time. A great evening."

The three walk to the sidewalk. Bob turns to Jack, reaches up, and puts his hand on the boy's shoulder. "Have a good day tomorrow, Jack. Grace, you as well. Thank you for the sandwich. Next time it's on me."

"See you soon, Bob Goeman!" Jack shouts as they walk away.

"Goodnight, Jack," Bob waves to the excited young boy.

Jack and Grace walk the last few blocks home.

"I enjoy talking to Bob. Can I call Dad when we get home?" Jack asks.

"Yes," Grace says, "and we're getting you a phone tomorrow. It'll be easier for you to call Dad that way. Maybe you'll even call me."

"I could call Lola too!" Jack shouts and jumps a little at the thought.

"If she'll give you her number," Grace teases.

Jack nods seriously. "Oh, I must ask her. What if she won't give me her phone number?"

"Jack, I am sure she will," Grace replies reassuringly.

"Mom, were you ever infatuated with Dad?"

The question breaks Grace's walk. She stumbles, and her shoulders slump over slightly. "Oh, you ask such good questions." She sighs, and they walk a long way before she answers. "I can't talk about that yet, but someday I'll tell you about it. For now…just know you're loved by both of us." Her voice is quiet and strained, her usual confident tone missing.

They walk the rest of the way without speaking. When they reach the front door, and as soon as they get inside, Grace hands Jack her phone.

"Here you go. Go ahead and bring your dad up to date."

Jack takes the phone and pushes a button. "Hi, Dad. Mom says she is getting me a phone tomorrow! I'm going to put Lola's name in it first…Of course, after yours and Mom's." Jack listens and takes a deep breath before answering his father's question, "Enjoy the journey? I don't see how I could enjoy the journey if she didn't even hold my hand. Bob says I am infatuated with Lola…Who is Bob? Bob stopped a man that tried to steal Mom's purse on the Metro. He has a strange accent and takes pictures of rats. The rat he had taken pictures of was nursing her young. You could see her mammary glands! Bob said he was sure that if the mother made it home that morning, the young would have been glad to see her. He says rats have emotions."

Jack continues to spew his newfound knowledge at an incredible speed to his father before he finally gives him a chance to talk. He looks up at his mom, still nodding, and hands the phone off to her.

"He wants to talk to you about Bob."

Grace takes the phone. "Hi, John. Yeah, Bob Goeman. Jack describes him accurately."

She continues to explain to John how Bob connected with Jack instantly. He was a different kind of man who had answers to every question and enjoyed taking pictures of anything and everything he was interested in. After a moment, Grace listens for John's response, and the expression on her face changes. "No, he's not interested in me that way. It's not like that at all." She listens again and grows impatient. "Of course, I'm sure, John. If any woman would know when a man was interested in her, you know I would."

She turns her back to Jack, who looks at her blankly, not knowing what his parents are talking about or why his mom is getting so upset. She wipes the corner of her eye quickly. "Yeah. I'll get Jack his phone tomorrow. I'll…have him give you updates on the hand-holding thing. Good night, John."

Grace hangs up the phone and sets it down. She takes a deep breath to collect herself, then asks, "What advice did your father give you about Lola?"

"He said, 'Enjoy the journey.' I'm not exactly sure what that means," Jack says, shrugging his shoulders. "What did he mean?"

"Well, there are no guarantees when it comes to relationships," Grace replies.

In an unusually quiet voice, Jack says, "I disagree."

Grace blinks. "What do you mean?"

"You will always be my mother."

"Jack," she sighs as she comes over to give him a quick hug, "you are sometimes wise beyond your years."

— 15 —

Saved

Bob makes his way home quickly. He opens the door, closes it gently behind him, and puts his camera bag on the kitchen counter. He pulls out a water bottle to sip on, walks over, and settles on the couch.

Just then, his phone rang. "Joint call: Danielle & Don" across the screen. Bob answers.

"What do you know, Danielle?"

"The President told his wife," she says quickly. "Confirmed. All of them. Chemical." there is a long breath after she talks, her voice soft, subdued, "Every one of them."

The phone silent for some time.

Finally, Bob asks, "What do you have, Don?"

"It is true. Found the weight of the warheads. They are lighter than before, using a glide path for dispersal. The rest is even worse. The United States is not the only power doing this. All the locations have reported. I can give you the details in the morning. It is bad. We need to act quickly."

"Don, do we have all their secrets? Locations? Bunkers? This will not work unless we have all their secrets."

Don's voice lightens and changes, almost jovial, "Oh, yes. We have all of them marked. No one can hide. If they are stupid enough to not listen, all will be equal for the first time. "Inalienable rights, all men are created equal," finally."

"We can track them, see them?" Bob asks.

"Yes, all of them."

"What about their communications? Can we breach?" Bob asks.

"Team needs a few more hours, the last detail. Some of the military systems are difficult, not impossible, of course. Just a little more time. The team will inform us when they are ready."

"Good. Until morning then. We hope morning comes. I am going to take a long walk, it might help me sleep. Good night Don. And Danielle, great work."

He puts his phone in his pocket and closes his eyes, sitting silently for a long time.

"There is a chance it could work. A good chance. It *could* work. There is no other way."

He grabs his phone again and heads out the door, down Main, walking briskly. People are on porch steps taking in the evening light. They say hello as he passes, and Bob smiles, then lowers his head as if in prayer, thinking how little they know, meditating as he walks, occasionally looking up at the night sky. He eventually finds himself in the business area of White Plains and stops at an alley for a brief rest.

"It is the man whose breath will not be a passing shadow," a voice says from the alley.

"Billy, you are a long way from the Metro." Bob turns to see Billy resting on a piece of cardboard behind a dumpster. Bob steps into the alley and walks over to Billy.

"Dumbass looking in the dumpster again," a voice scoffs. Bob turns slowly and faces the man who followed Grace pointing a gun at him. "Stop right there."

Bob walks towards him.

"I said stop! Don't you know what a gun is?" The man growls and shakes it.

"Yes, but I assume you want to talk to me before you shoot me." Bob's reply is calm and collected.

"Right, you are. Now, what were you looking for in the dumpster?"

"Information," Bob says.

"In a dumpster? You dumbass." The man tries again. "What does the woman know?"

"She only does computations on where the warhead is going, not what is in it."

"Who are you with?"

"I cannot tell you that."

"Do you know what is on the new warheads?"

"Yes."

"And why they changed?"

"Yes. And so much more; you would not be able to comprehend what I know. You want me to tell you, and of course I will not. You are doing what you are paid to do. So sad, like most here, following orders."

"Listen, wise guy, I'll ask you one more time, and then I'll shoot you in the knee," the man growls.

Bob turns to look over his shoulder and asks, "Billy, should I have him shoot me in the right or left?"

But Billy doesn't answer. Instead, he shouts, "I am your determined protector!"

The man glances towards the dumpster just as Bob's right arm swings. It hits the man's hand, deflecting the gun, and the shot goes wide. Bob's left fist rigidly rams into the man's throat just below his Adam's apple.

The gun drops to the ground, and the man struggles to try and catch his breath. Billy scampers out from behind the dumpster and picks up the gun. The man slumps to his knees, still wheezing and gasping. Bob stands in front of him.

Suddenly the man reaches behind and pulls a gun from his boot, Billy sees the gun and shoots. The man collapses.

He repeats shakily, "I am your determined protector." The body lays still, blood coming out of the temple. "'He shall not hunger or thirst anymore. God will wipe away his tears.' Isaiah 49:10." Billy drops the gun.

Bob goes over and looks at the man. "Gone. Died for nothing. Like so many of you here."

He digs through the man's pockets and locates his phone. "Let us leave this place, Billy," he says, "We were undetected. We do have this body, though."

"I...I've harvested this dumpster before. It's a once-a-week robotic pickup." Billy motions his head toward the dumpster. Spurred to action, he swings the lid open, gets in, and throws cardboard and trash on the ground. Billy scrambles back out and grabs the man by the feet. Bob holds the man's hands, and they hoist him into the dumpster. Billy throws the cardboard and trash on top of him and shuts the lid before getting his grocery cart.

"'For he will rescue us from every trap and protect us from deadly disease. He will cover us with his feathers. He will shelter us with his wings. His faithful promises are our armor and protection,' Psalm 91:2-4." Billy's voice cracks.

They leave the alley and walk up the street back towards White Plains. They pass a Chinese restaurant, and a young person exits a car, running in with an insulated box. Bob turns to Billy and beckons him to follow. They walk around the side of the car where the window is down, and Bob tosses the man's phone into the back seat. They walk on in silence.

Billy's words come out slowly, "I haven't killed another human being for over twenty years. There was...evilness about the man. I'd observed him for some time."

"I had never seen another human being killed deliberately before. I hope this is the last time. Who was he? Did he have children, a mate?" Bob wonders aloud.

"Yet, you may have made many things possible for me—for many—by killing him," Bob says. "I am thankful to still be here; to see what happens. There is still hope. Let us go break bread together."

"Yes, let us break bread together." Billy replies numbly and nods. " I never thought I would never kill anyone again. The woman...Grace. Is her information valuable to those seeking it?" Billy asks.

"The sad thing is, she has none."

"So, the man in the dumpster died for nothing?"

"Yes."

Billy stops walking and turns to look at him. "The information you have...everyone wants it?"

Bob stops a step later. "Yes."

"What are you going to do with it?"

"We may be able to change things."

"Things?"

"This world."

"Will there be weapons? Violence?" Billy's voice trembles again.

"No," says Bob. "We have no weapons."

"No weapons? And you keep saying 'we...'"

"I am not alone."

Billy looks at him, "Who are you, Bob Goeman?"

"I am your friend for keeps. Come on, Billy, let us get some food."

They walk in silence for several blocks.

Billy starts talking again. "I thought I could change things. I joined the military and killed innocent people. I've never forgiven myself. I don't know how to do that."

"Was it deliberate? Did you make that choice, or were you following orders?" Bob asks. "Why did your country go to war, and who decided? Did the people vote? How much of this guilt is yours?" Bob's questions are slow and deliberate.

"How many times I wish I'd never gone to war. The war changed nothing." Billy's voice breaks again, but he clears his throat as if to rid himself of showing emotion. Bob reaches over again and puts his hand on Billy's shoulder.

The traffic streams by them, and the streetlights light their way. Bob keeps his right hand firmly on Billy's shoulder as they walk until their pace slows and their steps match each other, slow step by step. Their heels touched the sidewalk precisely at the same time.

Billy stops walking, turns to Bob, and looks at him. "What...what am I feeling from you, Bob?" Billy reaches up and puts his hand on Bob's hand.

Bob shakes his head and says, "Just feel it."

They walk on, and Billy's posture slowly changes; his shoulders go back, and he stands tall. They stop at a streetlight. Bob's hand remains on Billy's shoulder, and together they look up at the sky, the stop light changing from red to yellow to green, many times as they stand still.

Then at the same time, they step forward as the light changes green. Their right foot touches the pavement at the same time. Bob removes his hand from Billy's shoulder.

They approach the sandwich shop and see that the lights are off, but the young boy from before sees Bob and smiles, turning the lights back on.

Bob and Billy both address him in Mandarin and give their thanks. Bob tells him to repeat what he had before. They sit down outside, in silence, just staring at each other.

"How did you do that...that...that feeling? What was that?" Billy asks quietly.

"A glimpse, just a glimpse of what is possible," Bob answers.

After a long moment, Billy says, "If you need help with your mission, I'm willing. Trying to change things without weapons...I'm all in."

"Thank you, Billy."

The food arrives. Billy reaches over, takes Bob's hands, and silently prays for a moment.

Billy notices the half sandwich, "Not hungry?"

"I had the pleasure of eating with Grace and Jack earlier. But I can always eat!" Bob takes a big bite from the sandwich and closes his eyes as he chews and swallows.

Billy watches. "You enjoy eating more than anyone I have ever seen," he says.

The moon rises over the sandwich shop as they eat and drink.

"Billy, are you from this city?" Bob asks, realizing he does not know much about the man before him.

"No. I'm from a small town in Kansas. I signed up for the search for WMDs. Then, when I got back to the States, I went home. They thought I was a hero. I couldn't stay there. Hero!" He scoffs. "People are so stupid! Hit the road, and now, here I am."

"Grace and Jack may need someone with a streetwise eye," Bob says and pointing his finger at Billy.

"Okay. What do I have to do?"

"Follow me," Bob says and stands up.

"Someone else said that a long time ago; they killed him."

Bob frowns. "I am not this world's Messiah." Billy just shrugs.

The two men walk on: the wheels squeak on the grocery cart.

Billy turns to Bob. "Where are we headed?"

"Where I currently lay my head to sleep."

"Do you hear it?" he asks, looking up.

"Hear what, Billy? I hear the wheel on your cart. What do you hear?" Bob asks curiously.

"I don't hear the wheel, only the universe."

"What does it say?"

"Something is going to happen. The universe will sing…or cry."

"Billy, who are *you*? How do you know these things?" Bob asks.

Billy just shakes his head. Eventually, the two reach the apartment.

"Here we are. Just push your cart in here."

"Billy, I have had a long day, so I will take the bedroom. You can use the couch. There is a washer and dryer in the utility room. The bathroom is stocked with towels. Take your time. I will be asleep in no time. Goodnight, Billy, make yourself at home."

With that, Bob goes into the bedroom and closes the door. He pulls out his phone and pushes a button. "Others are becoming desperate. I was followed and saved by a friend. It has to happen soon." He hangs up, kicks off his shoes, lays on the bed, and closes his eyes.

Billy takes his duffel bag into the utility room and puts all his clothes in the washer. He hesitates, then strips his clothes off and puts them in the washer too. Takes a zip-lock bag of toiletries out of his duffel bag, goes into the bathroom, and shuts the door.

The washer finishes spinning out as Billy comes out wrapped in a towel, clean-shaven. He takes the clothes out of the washer and starts the load in the dryer, then brings one of the chairs in from the small kitchenette to the utility room and sits by the dryer. Closes his eyes and leans back in the chair, waiting. When the dryer chimes, he takes his clean clothes out and dresses in the same clothes as before. Finally, he puts the rest of his clothes in the duffel bag and lays down on the couch.

"So good to feel clean," he mutters as he touches the still-warm clothes wrapped around his body. He is asleep in minutes.

He is in a dust storm, holding a rifle. Other men are with him having rifles. They point their rifles at the dust, the rifles fire, the empty shell casing, flying into the air, tumbling, floating, and falling to the ground. The men's faces are calm. A pile of empty cartridges is on the sand. The sound of metal on metal, the rifle clicking.

"I am empty, empty, empty," The men say in unison.

The men throw the rifles into the air. Their rifles fly into the air, tumble, over and over, and fall to the sand. They undress and drop their uniforms on the ground. Naked, they walk into the dust storm, the dust wraps around them, and they disappear.

Billy wakes up with a jolt when Bob comes out of the bedroom.

"Sleep okay?" asks Bob

"Had a dream."

"Want to tell me about it?"

"I was in a dust storm. The platoon all pointed our weapons at the dust. Usually, I have nightmares, you know, about the dead. The ones I killed. This one, though, wasn't a nightmare. This was…a *dream*." He recounts the dream, then adds, "All the guilt is not mine. I can't imagine the guilt the people have that ordered us there."

"The people that sent you there could not see. Insight, Billy, good for you," Bob says and then follows up with, "A question: how did you know to save me? You could have shot either of us or both."

"It was obvious. You carry no weapon. The woman, the boy, your concern for them. Your concern for me, 'stay away from that man.'" He hesitates before continuing too quickly, "And...I feel things. Some folks think I'm crazy. I know I'm not."

Billy stops and breathes. "You're...different. I feel something about you that I've never felt before. I can't describe it, though. You're good, I'm certain of that. You have a...calmness about you I have never seen before."

Bob says nothing and walks over to the kitchen cabinet. "Want some protein bars to take with you?" Bob throws them on the counter.

"No personal stuff in there," Billy nods. "You're on a mission. You travel light."

"Billy, I may need you for help, so I have some things to give you." Bob goes back into the bedroom and comes out with a small backpack. "There is a pre-paid phone in here and a charger. My phone number is there. There is also some cash."

He hands Billy the backpack. Billy takes the phone out first. "It'll take me a while to figure it out. I had a flip phone years ago. I'll try calling you later." Billy reaches into the bag, pulls out the envelope, looks in it, and blanches. "You don't have to pay or give me money."

"This is not a payment. Money has no value to me. Pass it on when you can."

Billy stares. "Thanks. What can I help you with?"

"The day may come when I need someone I can trust, someone with street smarts. You satisfy that on both counts. You have a phone now, and I will have a way to reach you."

"Does this have something to do with Grace and Jack?"

"Yes, and the rest of you."

"The rest?"

"If this works, you will see. How about a cup of coffee at Sam's?"

Billy grins, holding up the envelope. "Do you want a donut? Then it's my turn to buy."

They head out the door with Billy in the lead. After a bit, Billy timidly raises his hand and places it on Bob's shoulder.

Bob looks at him. "You have a question for me?"

"Are you ever going to tell me what your mission is?"

Bob just smiles. "I want a donut."

Billy shakes his head and laughs.

"Your mission today is to see if anyone is following Grace and Jack. I bet you will be invited to ride with them on the subway. Invited or not, you get on the train with them. When you get off, circle back and see if someone is tailing them. Find out if they have a new shadow."

"I can manage that. What do I do if they are being followed?

"Call me first, stay with them, keep them safe. I will get you help."

Billy nods.

"Great. Just give me a call when you know if we have a new person to worry about," says Bob. "What else do you have going on today, Billy?"

"Thought I would check in at the VA and the homeless shelter. Thinking of trying something new."

"New is good."

They step up to Sam's. "Good morning, Sam. Two of your excellent coffees for my friend Billy and me. I would like a donut as well."

"Coming up," says Sam, "Billy, what do you take in your coffee?"

"Oh, I love sugar. Four, please."

"Sugar! You people all gather together," Sam laughs as he puts everything on the counter. "Two coffees, four sugars in each, and one donut."

Billy pulls out a twenty and puts it on the counter. "Here you are. My treat today."

Bob smiles at the generosity. He takes the donut and eats quickly before saying, "Got to run, going to run to the airport and pick up a friend. Billy—Jack and Grace should be along soon. Tell them hello and that I will see them at the school."

"You got it. I am your determined protector."

Bob nods and walks away.

Sam watches from behind the counter and asks, "So, Billy, how do you know Bob?"

"Well, it started when he gave me money. I gave him something in return. It's a long story, not enough time this morning to tell you. I can tell you, we are now friends for keeps." Billy grins widely at Sam.

Sam smiles and touches the crucifix under his t-shirt. "There's something about him that's...different."

"Yes, yes, there is."

"Do you know what it is?"

Billy shrugs. "The universe may sing."

— 16 —

Makeup and Pimples

Jack wakes up early, rolls over, and gets out of bed. In the bathroom, Jack looks in the mirror and sees a new pimple.

"No! Not another one! It's so gross."

He dresses and goes downstairs to the kitchen, grabbing the Chocolate Chex, milk, and bowl. Jack crunches away to himself as Grace walks into the kitchen and starts her usual coffee.

"Good morning, Jack," she says as she comes over and puts her hand on his shoulder.

"Good morning, Mom. Do you think Bob will become your boyfriend?"

Grace splutters. "Oh, no! No, no, it'll be a *long* time for that kind of move. I mean, it's an excellent question, and I did ask him to join us yesterday. But no, I find him... *interesting*, and well, I do not know. There's something quite different about him, but it's not like that."

"I didn't think so," Jack says with a shrug. "Just thought I would ask."

"It's okay. What do you think of Bob?"

"He listens. I mean, he *listens*. I feel no judgment from him. There's just something quite different about him. I don't know, just a *feeling*. His accent, the way he walks. So graceful! I feel like a horse stomping beside him!" Jack laughs, then sober. "I got a new zit. So gross." He takes another massive bite of cereal.

"You look fine," Grace assures him, then she stands. "I'm going to get ready for work. Be down in a few minutes. Bob'll be at Sam's this morning."

She goes upstairs and stands in front of the mirror, looking at her face, studying her eyes and minor imperfections only she notices. She applies her usual makeup; her morning routine is second nature at this point. She lets her mind wander so much that she doesn't notice Jack standing outside her bathroom, watching her with a puzzled look.

"Mom, you know you're pretty, right? You don't need to spend so much time on your face," he says.

"Thank you for the compliment," Grace smiles before digging into her makeup bag and pulling out her signature lipstick.

"No, really, you don't have to. Lola uses just a little bit of lipstick, and that's it. Why do you use so much?"

She glances in the mirror one last time, trying to ignore Jack's question. "Let's go, Jack. We'll be late."

They're out the door in a few moments, walking to the Metro and Sam's. Sam's cheerful voice greets them. "Good morning, Grace and Jack!"

"Hi, Sam!" Jack booms.

Another man is standing at the counter with a cup of coffee. "Good morning, you two!" Billy greets them.

"Good morning, Billy. You look great!" Grace says as she admires his newly clean appearance.

"You shaved," Jack says with a grin and touches his own face.

"Yes, I did. I had a sleepover with Bob last night."

"Sleepover?" Grace asks.

"Yes, we ran into each other last night. He was out for a walk and offered me his shower and couch." Billy smiles at them.

"Well, you look fantastic! So where is our mutual friend this morning?"

"He had to pick up someone named Don at the airport. Left about fifteen minutes ago. He got a phone call late last night."

"Aw, I hoped we would see him so he could quiz Jack on the mysterious menu at the school later today. Jack won't tell me anything!" Grace laughs before turning back to Sam. "Can you hook me up with some coffee, please? Jack, do you need anything?"

"I'm good to go. Ready to get to school. Helping with the meal we're serving after school today to the parents."

"So what's the menu?"

"It's a surprise," Jack insists. "Something you have never had before!" He wiggles around in excitement and covers his mouth like he's trying to keep the secret.

Grace reaches into her purse to pay Sam, but before she can open her wallet, Billy hands Sam a ten-dollar bill with a smile.

"My honor." He smiles, white teeth showing.

Grace smiles in return. "Thank you, Billy! I'm so glad you and Bob had some time together. What do you think of him?" Billy's face is so different, she thinks. His demeanor, how he stands tall and confident, it's as if he's a new person.

Billy nods slowly as he speaks. "A friend is always loyal, and a brother born to help in time of need. A verse from Proverbs. Bob is my friend for keeps."

"What's different about him, do you think? I've been trying to figure that out," Sam says.

"I like the differences!" Jack interjects.

"I like them too," Sam agrees. "I've handed coffee to thousands of people. I can't put my finger on it." His voice trails off, and he rubs something under the collar of his t-shirt; the outline of the crucifix is noticeable if you're paying attention.

Billy is paying attention.

Sam sees him looking. Just for a moment, they look at each other.

Then Grace says, "Thanks, Sam. Billy, have a good day. If you see Bob before we do, tell him hello."

"I will. Are you going to White Plains?" Billy asks.

"Yes, we are."

"So am I. There's something I want to check on there."

"Billy, come with us!" Jack says excitedly.

"I'd like that. I'd like that very much."

"Yes, please join us, Billy," Grace adds.

They walk to the Metro. They almost look like a family of three; the confident man walking with his beautiful wife, the toe-walking son falling slightly behind.

"Do you hear it?" Billy asks as they enter the station.

"Hear what?" Jack asks.

"Sometimes the universe sings to me. This morning, I hear it."

"The planet is turning while it's moving through space. It does make a sound!" Jack exclaims.

Billy looks at him, slightly shocked, and shakes his head with a grin.

They find a place to sit, Grace by the window, Jack in the middle, and Billy on the outside.

"What exactly does Bob do?" Grace asks Billy. "I know he takes pictures, but I never figured out exactly how he makes a living."

"He inherited some money. That's what he told me last night. Very generous, too. He gave me some funds. I told him I would never be able to pay him back."

"What did he say?"

"He told me I would pass it on someday."

The train rolls out of the station.

"So, where are you headed in White Plains?" Grace asks.

"The Veterans Center. Going to check on some work things. After my evening with our mutual friend, I'm ready to try something new."

Grace's face changes, oddly somber, and she looks at Billy. "Hope it goes well for you, Billy."

"Thanks." Billy straightens and turns. "Enough about me, though. Jack, what is the meal you're serving at school?"

"We're sworn to secrecy!" Jack replies.

"I see. Can you give us a hint, maybe? Vegetables? Meat? Bread?" Billy asks.

"Nope, not going to talk about it," Jack says, snickering again.

"Are all of you cooking?"

"Yes, we're teams for different parts of the meal. Lola and I are on the same team."

"Ah, sounds delicious," Billy laughs.

The train rolls into White Plains station slowly. When it stops, they stand up, exit, and make their way to the sidewalk.

"The V.A. is up that way. Thank you for the company," Billy nods at them.

"Our pleasure, have a wonderful day," Grace says as she reaches over and touches his shoulder.

They go their separate ways. Billy gets about a block away, circles behind them, and follows, staying out of their view. He does this for blocks, stopping in doorways, watching, and looking. Finally, he walks away from them, pulls his phone out, and dials a number.

"No one is following them. When are you going to tell me who you are?"

All Done

Bob pulls up at the arrival area of the airport. Don opens the back door, throws in his backpack, and gets in the front seat. He pants lightly, out of breath.

"Coffee. The airport coffee is terrible. The air is starting to get to me." Don wheezes.

"Sam has the best coffee. We will get you a real cup of coffee. The air though...well, you know." Bob accelerates into the traffic aggressively, causing a slew of cars to lay on their horns. "You go first. I will talk after we are on the freeway."

"We discovered in their data that the weight of the warheads has decreased. Used the same fibers for recording. The United States of America have changed their warheads. It is chemical. Death in ninety seconds. There are no nuclear weapons except hypersonic offensive weapons for destroying launch sites. The hypersonic ones are all on alert. The rest is even more unsettling."

"I'm listening."

"The rest of them are doing it, too. The whole world's weaponry is changing. So what are they going to do with all that plutonium?" Don says, sarcasm in his voice, "The stupidity."

Bob listens silently as he floors the accelerator, and the car enters the freeway. He joins the throng of cars and finds a lane without issue.

Don continues, "The President did not go into complete detail with his wife, only telling her it was chemical, and they would be safe in their bunker. Danielle sent me the recording. I call it, 'The First Lady curses.'"

Don pushes buttons on his phone. "Chemical! Craig, what about all the children? And we would be in the bunker, safe and snug. How fucked up is that?" a woman's voice shouts.

"Carla, it's to show our strength," a second, male voice replies in a more even tone.

"*Bullshit*. Killing children!" The first scoffs. "Strength? How God damn strong do you have to be to kill innocent children?"

Don ends the audio and puts his phone back in his pocket. Bob nods his head to himself, processing the information.

"There is much more to the fight. He slept on the couch. There may never be roses in the bedroom again." He pauses, "I hope there are."

They are silent for a long time.

"What happened here?" Don finally asks.

"I went for a walk after a pleasant evening meal with Grace and Jack. I passed an alley entryway; a homeless man, Billy, was sitting by a dumpster. He greeted me. Then out of nowhere, the man who has been following Grace and Jack has a gun in my face."

"The same man that saw you at the dumpster from before?"

"Yes. The man wanted to know what the warheads were being replaced with. He wanted to know what Grace

knew. He wanted to know what I found in the dumpster. There was a struggle. I knocked the man's gun to the
ground. As the man was reaching for another gun in his
boot, Billy grabbed the gun on the ground and shot him in
the temple. Billy saved me."

Bob changes lanes quickly and accelerates again.

"So, who was this man who followed you and Grace?"

"Unknown. We assume working for another country that wants to know why the United States is changing
their warheads."

"What did you do with the body?"

"He will end up in a landfill somewhere. He is currently at the bottom of a large dumpster. Billy informed me
it is a weekly robotic pickup."

"What happened afterward?"

"Billy and I walked. He talked. He went to war and
accidentally killed innocent people. I listened; he is better."

Don nods his head affirmingly. "So many wounded
soldiers here. Glad you got to help one. Who does he think
you are?" Don asks.

"Billy told me he knows I am on a mission, and he
heard the man ask me about the warheads. He is trust-
worthy. No, he is more than that. He is a friend and, in some
ways, psychic; Billy knows something is going to happen."

"So, are we done?" Don asks.

"Yes, we have it all. We are ready. It will happen in the
next twenty-four hours," Bob says.

"If any other powers discover this, they might launch
first strike," Don says.

"Choosing sides, like children," Bob says shaking his head.

"Chemical. Just kill the people. Guns in holsters. So
many weapons you can see them from space, yet they are
trying to keep them secret! Breathing devices. The plankton
is dying. This traffic is six lanes wide. Bob, look at them.

Swerving between lanes, horns honking, all acting like to-morrow is a sure thing."

They are silent for the rest of the drive. They exit the freeway and soon are in the Bronx, on 124th street. Bob pulls up to the garage door and opens it. The car pulls in, and they get out.

"Okay, are you good here, Don? Jack and Grace invit-ed me to this special dinner the kids are doing at school." Bob says. He stops, then says, "I want to see them again." He stops again, and breathes in. "You are a great partner. Glad you were with me for this."

"Until tomorrow?" Don replies.

"We hope so. Yes, we hope so."

They walk towards each other, stop, and look di-rectly into each other's eyes. The two of them still. They stand that way for some time, reach out and, put hands on each other's shoulders, then nod their heads in silent un-derstanding.

Bob walks to his car. Don follows and watches him back out of the garage as he pulls away.

— 18 —

The Journey Begins

There is a knock on Grace's office door.

"Yes, come on in," she calls.

"You're working late tonight. It's after four," Wayne says as he steps in and shuts the door behind him.

"There's a dinner tonight at the school. It doesn't start until five, so I'm just spending the time working," she explains, "Jack won't give me a clue about the menu. Said it's a secret." She smiles, thinking of how silly her son has been acting about this meal.

"I think I've heard about this from some other parents in the past," says Wayne, "The students pick a menu that's supposed to reflect our world. It's always different."

"I invited Bob to join us," Grace adds, "Thanks for your advice on friends. Jack and I find him...stimulating."

"Well, enjoy your evening, Grace. Hope I get to meet Jack someday." With that, Wayne steps out again.

Grace shuts off the lights and leaves her office. She collects her phone, goes through security, and exits the building. She walks up to the school's entrance to find Herschel standing outside, greeting parents as they come.

"Hello, Grace! Ready for the most interesting meal you have ever had?" Herschel's grin spreads wide across his face.

"Yes!" Grace laughs, "Jack has been quite mysterious about this. Oh, and Bob Goeman will be coming in a bit to join me. Jack and I invited him."

"I will keep an eye out for him."

Grace thanks Herschel and walks down the hallway. She sees a young girl with a poster that says, "Welcome."

Grace smiles at her. "Good afternoon, young lady."

"Hello," the girl says, then points. "The program is straight down the hallway. When you get to the end, turn right."

Grace does as directed and enters the cafeteria.

"Grace De Falco, welcome!" Miss Alana calls from the entrance.

"Miss Alana," Grace says with a wave, "so happy you're here."

"Jack is doing great," Miss Alana says, and Grace's smile grows.

"This is an amazing school. You've done things with Jack in a few days that I didn't think were possible. Thank you."

"Here is your name badge," says Miss Alana with a pleased nod, "You can pick any table. We'll be serving in about ten minutes. "

Grace goes to one of the small, round tables. She picks a chair, sits down, and greets the three other people sitting there. The table has bowls set at each seat with a spoon, a small plate, and a water glass. In the middle of the table is a bowl with a small amount of uncooked rice and lentils. The people around the table are trying to ignore it but keep glancing at it, wondering if this is the meal for tonight.

A man directly across the table smiles at Grace. "My name's Fred Alonzo, and this is my wife, Monica."

"I'm Vonda Alvarez," a plump woman sitting by herself chimes in.

"Hello, I'm Grace De Falco. Its nice they put our child's name on our badges. Vonda, what can you tell me about Luke?"

"Oh, he's amazing. He looks at a calendar once and remembers all the dates and holidays! He can do complex puzzles quickly and learned chess overnight. He even makes up his own codes. Sometimes it is like he is somewhere else." Vonda says, then asks, What about Jack?"

"Knee goes ninety miles an hour up and down," Grace laughs. "When he reads something, he remembers at least 90% of it. Misses some social clues and talks tons. I worry that people can find him annoying. The school is giving him more confidence." She looks at the other parents and lands on the woman across from her, "Monica, tell me about your daughter."

"Jena crawled up on a piano bench when she was four and started playing. I cannot carry a tune. They say she's a savant," Monica says, then somberly, "I feel overwhelmed sometimes. Inadequate. How can I guide her? But she's so brilliant. She sees the notes as colors. Can you imagine? Colors?" Moncia takes a moment and then looks down. "Sorry, I started rattling on."

"May I join you?" Bob waves as he pulls out a chair.

"You made it! Thanks for coming." The smile on Grace's face grows, and she motions for the chair and introduces Bob to everyone. Fred studies Bob's name badge with a handwritten name on it.

"You new here, Mr. Goeman?" he asks.

"Yes. I am a friend of Jack and Grace," Bob replies.

Ms. Alana stands at the front of the hall and gathers everyone's attention. "Good evening!" They look up to see her holding a small microphone.

"Thank you for coming. Each year we have done different things for this event based on what the children are learning in social studies. This year, the discussions focused on climate and, of course, crop production. We asked the students what can be done about it now. What they are about to serve is the option that received the most votes when our students were asked to choose the menu for the evening. The children are ready now, so please, enjoy!" With that, Ms. Alana sits down.

The students come in carrying pots of soup, occasionally giggling as they serve. They put one ladle of soup in each bowl. Other students come out with stacks of bread, putting one slice on the plate. They finish serving and all go to a table at the front of the room and sit down.

"Please eat and enjoy. When your bowl is empty, if you want more, please raise your hand. The soup bowl will be filled one more time, so enjoy each spoonful." Ms. Alana seems to chuckle along with the kids as she sits down.

Lentils and rice float in the beef broth. Bob picks up his spoon and takes a sip of his soup. Grace, the Alonzos, and Vonda join him. They eat in silence, the spoons clanking on the bowl.

Around the room, people are quiet. Occasionally, you can hear someone say, "exceptionally good soup," and, "They used beef broth, and no butter for the bread?"

The students work the room, putting in the second ladle full of soup as necessary and refilling the water glasses. Eventually, Miss Alana stands up again and begins speaking.

"This meal is around six hundred calories. According to research, the average man needs around two thousand calories per day to survive, and the average woman only slightly less. In many countries, there are lines of people with bowls waiting for this. You and I will be hungry when we have finished our meal. When we have finished eating, the children will answer questions."

The sounds of the spoons tapping the sides of the bowls continue. Finally, the spoon tapping is silent.

"I am curious what other topics you voted on?" a voice from one table asks.

"Who would like to answer that question?" Ms. Alana asks. A familiar hand shoots up quickly, waving in the air frantically. "Yes, Jack De Falco. Please answer the question."

Jack stands up, his hand flipping, his body moving, highly animated. "Cleaning up the oceans and the atmosphere. The ocean is full of plastic, and we all know what the air is like. We're breathing purified air in this building. The planet's oxygen levels are decreasing. People use devices to help them breathe," Jack's voice boomed out over the crowd.

"Thank you, Jack," Miss Alana says as Jack steps back. She scans the crowd. "Another question?"

A hand goes up at another table, "I understand what you are saying about the calories; Americans overeat. What are you suggesting we do, though, eat less?" a woman asks.

This time, a couple of hands go up amongst the kids.

"Lola McGregor. You want to try and answer that question?"

"Yes," Lola says. "Certainly, eating less would help. In time, there could be more food for others. Sharing our food would also help, though. The United States is one country that has food surpluses, but we're not sharing. Food is rationed in some countries, but not here, so we could send food to help countries where unpredictable weather disrupts food production."

"Thank you, Lola," says Miss Alana. "We hope you leave here with a new insight into our world today and think of things you can do. Be proud of these children. They want to make this world a better place. Please visit amongst yourselves about this subject. You can have dessert while you're visiting." She motions to the children.

The children start laughing as they bring over transparent glass bowls filled with LifeSavers candies and, using tongs, place one on each of the plates. People pick them up and put them in their mouths. Many of the parents are smiling, some laughter in the room.

"The children could have picked any candy, but they decided on LifeSavers. Right now, children are starving." Miss Alana pauses, looking around the room, taking the LifeSaver, holding it in her hands as if it is a communion wafer. "When you put the candy in your mouth, it tastes sweet. They're such a simple thing, just one piece of candy. Millions would shriek with joy to have this." She stops for a moment and stands in silence.

"This idea came out of your children's minds." Ms. Alana says before sitting down, and parents start to applaud, smiling at each other.

"So, Bob, what did you think of the meal, or rather, the message from these young people?" Mr. Alonzo asks.

Bob answers, "Hopeful; the children are trying to lead us. The innocence and hope, believing that everyone would share. The more I think about it, the more moved I become. Children see reality. I am thankful I was here."

"Me too!" Mr. Alonzo says, "It was amazing. I was looking at the lentils and rice when we arrived. Think of it. That is what people are looking forward to. They're thankful to get it."

"Six hundred calories isn't enough. You all can see I'm not a size two," Vonda says with a hint of an amazed laugh, "Some of us have too much, and others too little. Children always know the truth."

Ms. Alana stands up, "You can collect your children and head home. I'm available to visit with any of you if you'd like to chat."

"We're going to give our best to Ms. Alana. Nice meeting you all," says Mr. Alonzo as he and his wife leave.

"So glad I came. We've got so much in common! I hope to see you all again. Who knows, maybe I'll be one size smaller." With that, Ms. Alonzo also stands up and leaves.

"There is a question, of course, about the food shortages."

"What is the question?" Bob looks at her.

"How did the world get here? Some with so much, some with so little," Grace says quietly.

There is a line of parents that are saying goodbye to Ms. Alana. Grace gets in the line, and Bob stands with her. Children come and stand by their parents, visiting and chatting excitedly.

"Mom, Bob, what did you think?" Jack says, shaking his wrist in excitement as he comes over.

"Jack, you were outstanding. I'm so proud of you!" Grace exclaims, hugging her son.

Jack grins. "I was so nervous, but the school has helped me. Bob, what did you think of the message?"

"Excellent, Jack," Bob smiles.

"You should have heard all the discussions after we studied the calorie intake of the different countries. It is so sad. It makes you wonder what will happen to everyone," Jack says.

"Questions Jack, questions. Keep asking questions. You never know where those are going to lead."

They make their way up the line and finally reach Ms. Alana.

"This is amazing. Everyone wants to thank her." Grace says.

"Yes. There is a community here," Bob says quietly. "Thank you so much for your work with Jack," Grace gushes.

"You're so welcome," Ms. Alana says, "We have a great staff."

"Ms. Alana, this is Bob Goeman. He's a friend of ours."

Ms. Alana extends her hand to Bob, and they shake hands. The bracelet on Bob's wrist is visible, and she admires it momentarily.

"Welcome, Bob. That's an interesting bracelet. The symbols are so unique."

"Yes. A gift I received a long time ago."

"We'll let the rest of the people say hello," Grace says as she shakes Ms. Alana's hand. Jack just smiles and bounces up and down to himself.

They walk out of the school, past Herschel saying, "Have a good night!"

They are standing at the crosswalk, waiting for the light to change, when Jack speaks. "I was so nervous, but I was able to do it. I never believed I could do something like that."

"I am so proud of you," Grace repeats, still in awe of how well her son is doing.

"Mom, the school is helping me," Jack repeats, "We all work together, and we are a team. Everyone keeps saying that we can do anything."

"Speaking of anything, how are things with Lola?" Bob asks.

Jack grins, "We…" He is interrupted by a large, loud construction truck rattling through the intersection, loaded with broken-up concrete, the metal bed banging, and dust flying. "We got to help put the soup together in the kitchen. We opened the beef broth and dumped it in."

"You did not volunteer any information about the hand-holding," Bob smiles at him.

"The right time has not happened yet. It was fun just working together," Jack grins.

They cross the street together, dust still in the air from the construction truck.

"Grace, your day?" Bob asks.

"Nothing new; still working on the same project. After watching the staff at the school, I wonder…well, I wonder what I am doing." She pauses. "They're all so happy, on fire with enthusiasm for what they do."

Bob turns and looks at her, "You are asking yourself some important questions."

"Yes, yes, I am. Ms. Alana loves her job, Herschel and all the teachers do."

The three reach the construction site just as a front-end loader scoops broken bricks from the sidewalk. A man on the machine looks their way.

"STOP! Give me a minute. I need to move these. Just take a second!" He grins as he shouts. They stand and wait, the scoop pushed under the broken bricks as the operator raises the scoop.

A sound erupts from the street, like metal crashing, and the three turn to see a cement truck crash into the side of a UPS truck, sending it hurtling toward them.

There is no screaming; instead, time stands still. Bob turns to Grace and Jack, touches the bracelet on his wrist, and throws his arms around them with his back to the street. The man on the front-end loader jumps off to the sidewalk on the other side.

The truck speeds towards them. The front tires jump the curb. Bob's left arm is around Grace, her eyes open wide. Jack's face is above Bob's right arm. Both look at the truck barreling toward them. They scream. Bob holds them tight.

Then…*light*.

There is light around them, bright and clear. A sound, a beautiful single note unlike anything heard on earth, rings out around them.

The UPS truck hits the light and stops.

Bob looks at Grace. He reaches his hand to her face, the palm flat on her cheek, the fingers tracing the cheek very slowly. She is staring at him, her eyes wide, her mouth moving, but no words come out. His fingers reach the bottom of her face and lift slowly. Grace inhales sharply and gasps.

Bob looks at Jack. Jack has tears coming out of his eyes, but he is not crying, he is just staring at Bob. "How? *How*?!"

Bob says nothing, just smiles at Jack.

Then the light stops.

"Mom! Are you ok?!" Jack shouts at Grace.

Grace nods her head but says nothing.

Bob turns around to face the truck. The engine hisses, clanks, then stops. On the dash of the truck is a camera, its red light blinking. Seeing the camera, he turns to look at Grace and Jack again.

"There is a camera in the truck; this may have been filmed. If it was, they will be looking for me."

"What do you mean, 'they?' Who-what are you? What was that light? What did I hear?!" Grace's voice trembles.

"Grace, leave now! Now! They will want you too. Call me when you are alone," Bob shouts and begins to sprint away from the scene. His feet barely touch the sidewalk.

Jack watches him intently, his eyes locked until Bob turns the corner at the end of the block and disappears from view.

The driver gets out of the truck.

Grace walks over to him. "Are you okay?"

"Yeah, yeah, just shaken up. The other truck hit me so hard I couldn't reach the brake. How about you?"

"We're...we're fine."

"What the hell stopped the truck?! Something stopped the truck. Some guy was holding you. Where did he go? There was light... What did you see?" The driver asks insistently, eyes wide.

"I...I don't know," Grace mumbles, shaking her head back and forth, "I don't know."

The front-end loader operator comes around the back of the truck to the sidewalk, brushing debris off his clothing.

"Wow, I thought you were toast! I had to jump. What stopped the truck? Lady, you and your son were in front of it. What stopped the truck?!"

Grace says nothing; she's still trying to think about how logically they could have avoided death.

A police officer pulls up and gets out of his car. "Does anyone need an ambulance?" he asks, his voice frantic.

"Just a tow truck," the truck driver replies numbly, wide eyes staring at Grace's blank face.

"How about you, lady? Are you okay? How about the boy?" the officer asks, perplexed.

"We're fine, but I don't know about the other driver out there in the street," says Grace.

The police officer walks over to the other driver and starts talking to him. Another police car arrives to direct traffic. Grace nods at Jack, and in confusion, they walk away. When they get around the corner and stop, Grace grabs her son and hugs him for a long time.

"We almost died," Grace says, tone calm despite the shaking in her voice.

"How did he *do* that, Mom?" Jack asks, "Who is he? Where did that light come from? I was covered with goosebumps and warm at the same time, and that note, that tone, it was so beautiful. Did you hear it, or feel it? That feeling of being...of being...what was it?"

"Like a thousand...hugs, for want of a better word. What was it? It was more than just Bob. Around me, holding me. It was a feeling of being safe." She shakes herself, trying to be practical. "Come on, Jack, we're going home. We're not taking the train, though. I'm calling a cab."

"Mom, what do you think Bob meant when he said, 'They will be looking for me, for us?'" Jack asks as Grace calls for a cab, but she shakes her head again.

"How would I know? I'm just as confused as you are. The truck was coming right at us, and he grabbed us. There was a light, and the truck stopped."

"Mom, who do you think he is?"

She thinks for a moment before replying, "When the truck was coming, he was holding me, his arm around me. Then the light. The sound…when it was over and he reached and touched my face, it…it…I don't know."

She stops, shaking her head.

"What do you mean you don't know?" Jack asks.

"His fingers traced across my cheek, yet it was…it wasn't *physical*. I'm not sure what it was."

"There is our cab," Jack says.

The cab pulls over and they get in. "Where to?"

"9808 Mill, White Plains." Grace pauses and looks at her son., then adds, "Don't break any laws or anything, but the faster, the better."

The cabby nods. "ten minutes." He moves into the traffic of the night, keeping his word and moving quickly.

They're silent the whole drive. When they reach the apartment, Grace pays the cab driver, and they hustle up the stairs and shut the door. Grace locks it, shaking her head. She sits on the couch, takes her phone, and pushes a button.

"John, it's Grace. Listen, Jack and I were…Bob stopped a truck somehow…No, it was out of control, coming right for us and…and…What if something had happened? We were almost killed, it…" She starts sobbing.

Jack comes over and sits beside her, taking the phone from her. "Bob saved us! A light stopped a truck! There was this truck coming right at us, but then this light wrapped around us. The truck stopped! There was also a sound, a note, a hum." Jack stops and listens, "I *cannot* calm down. This made no scientific sense! Bob stopped a truck from killing us somehow with a light. This is not explainable, logical, or possible!" He listens to his dad again and sighs. "Sure, I'll put Mom back on."

Grace takes a moment to compose herself, then explains the situation, from the dinner to the construction yard and the crash. There is a long pause before she responds to John. "No, Bob's a man, not an angel...I know you have your faith, but Bob...Bob is just a man, a human being." She stops and listens for some time. "Listen, we're going to try to sleep. John, be ready to come to the city, please. I'll call you when I know more. Bob said the camera in the truck may have filmed everything. If so they will be looking for him." She hangs up.

"So, what did Dad think?" Jack sits beside her, and she puts her arm around him. He leans his head on her chest.

"Well," Grace says slowly, "an Angel was your dad's first choice. You know your dad, Catholic and all that. 'Anything is possible,' he kept saying, 'God's power,' etc. Then he said something that totally surprised me! He suggested an extraterrestrial, like a good alien. As strange as it sounds...I think the odds favor alien."

Jack sits back up. "Mom, think about the rat. Why was he so fascinated with one rat? There are millions of them. If he is not from here, maybe he had never seen one before! And did you see how he ran? His feet barely touched the ground."

"I remember that first morning on the train," Grace says, "when he talked about mammals on this little blue dot. Who talks about us like that? He's not from here, he can't be, but the big question is *why* is he here?" She thinks again, then says, "He seemed very interested in my job. Seemed to be trying to get information without asking for it."

"He listened to me, like no one has ever listened," Jack says, unusually quiet. "He heard every word, connecting to me. Not judging me for how I am—my toe walking, repeating phrases, obsession with data, history, questions, and my loud voice. Bob listens. I love that."

Grace looks at him, heart aching. "Yeah, I think I understand. I've learned so much from him."

"Light does not have power," Jack says, seeming to shake himself. "Was the light a product of some power that Bob used? What was the note? How could it make you feel so safe, so good? Telepathy? Telekinesis? He touched his bracelet as he was turning. Did the note have power? What does that mean? Did the sound, the note have power? What does that mean?" Jack's hand flips rapidly.

Grace pulls out her phone again, dials a number. "I got his voice mail," she murmers. Then, at a normal volume, "Bob, we're home. I'll...I'll leave my phone on." She hangs up and hugs Jack one more time. "Come on, we need to try and sleep."

"What do you think is going to happen tomorrow? Bob said 'they' will want us too."

"I don't know what's going to happen tomorrow," says Grace. After a moment, she adds, "I'm not afraid, though. Are you?"

"No, no, I am not. You are right, we need some rest, but how can I quit thinking about this and sleep?"

They both walk to their bedrooms. As Jack gets to his door, he says, "Mom, you gasped when he touched your face."

"Yes, I did. Like I said, it wasn't physical, yet it was...I'm still thinking about what it meant, what I felt."

Jack nods, considering. "Goodnight Mom."

"Good night, Jack." Grace shakes her head, muttering to herself, "Tomorrow, tomorrow, tomorrow! How am I going to sleep?"

In a tone of his voice that she had never heard before, Jack says, "What is possible has changed forever."

— 19 —

Yes Father, A Light

"My God Grace, who is he, what is he? Please let me know when you know more." John De Falco slips his phone into his pocket and walks around the room. "Bob Goeman, who are you? What are you? You saved Jack and Grace." He puts his hand to his mouth as if holding back a sob.

He paces the study; shelves on one side hold hundreds of books. A desk, lamp, papers, and computer. He sits down in an easy chair.

He pulls out his phone and pushes a number. "Good evening, Father. I apologize for calling this evening. I have an emergency. Can you meet me at St. Mary's?"

In a few minutes, he is at the chapel; he pulls up in front and parks beside a red 1980 Triumph. "Forgive me, God, I speed." proclaims a bumper sticker. He walks up the steps to the main entrance and walks to the confession booth.

"Forgive me, Father. It has been two weeks since my last confession." John sighs; there is a long period of silence.

"Grace called me. Something happened. Grace and Jack were saved from almost certain death by a light that surrounded them as they were held by a—" John stops. Silence. Then he continues. "They were held by a man. The light somehow stopped a truck."

"Repeat that; a light?" The voice loud, credulous.

"Yes, Father, a light."

"Tell me exactly what Grace said in the phone call."

John relates the phone call.

"So, Jack also said the same thing."

"Yes."

"Who is this man?"

"His name is Bob Goeman. Grace met him on the streets of New York. He was taking pictures of a rat. Thinks he is a photographer. Strange, different. Connected to Jack's difference in a few sentences. Evidently has a gift of listening intently. He also stopped a man from stealing her purse, tripping him somehow."

"Are they, they involved."

"No."

"Are you sure?"

"Yes."

"John, considering the state of your relationship with Grace, do you think she could have made this up? Do you think this could be a cry for help?"

"Grace has lied to me before, but this was real. Grace cried on the phone. Grace does not cry. She cried! On the phone! And Jack...Jack, at this point in his development, does NOT lie. Remember, Jack has some spectrum issues. I don't think he can lie. He would see a lie as unscientific."

"John, John. Let us sit here in silence for just a few minutes. Please be still with me."

The seconds tick by, then a few minutes.

The voice from behind the screen speaks first.

"John, here is what we know to be true. Your ex-wife, who does not express emotions easily, cried on the phone. Your son, who does not lie, confirms the same thing happened to him. A truck speeding towards them was stopped by light while this man held them."

"Yes. That is my analysis too. My first thought was Angel; now I am leaning towards 'not from here.'"

"Why, not an Angel?"

"Grace said she was held by a man when the truck came at them."

"A light, a light. My God, Oh! I wish I had been there. Are you going?" The voice asks.

"Yes, Father. In the morning, plan to leave around four o'clock, beat the traffic."

"At your last confession, you talked about Grace and your pain. How is that going?"

"Still there."

"You have been given a miracle. Maybe the light will help you."

"Maybe Father, maybe."

"John, concentrate on what has happened. Imagine if you were there with them."

"Thank you, Father, for coming on short notice."

"I will never forget this confession. How am I going to sleep? Say it with me."

"Hail Mary..."

They finish, the voice behind the screen, "I have something I thought of just now. From the Book of Isaiah: 'Arise, shine; for thy light has come, and the glory of the LORD is risen upon thee.' Safe travels John."

Buying a Disguise

Bob sprints away from the truck, leaving Grace and Jack staring after him. He turns around at the corner and looks back. Sees the driver emerge from the truck to talk to Grace and Jack, then look down the street towards him. Bob turns the corner and walks as fast as he can without drawing any more attention to himself. He pulls out his phone.

"Billy, I need your help. I need a place where there are no cameras." He listens. "The alley? Okay. And I need a disguise. Do you have some old clothes and a hat?" He listens again for a moment. "Okay, I will get a cab. Be there in a few minutes."

Bob hails a cab, gets in, and gives the driver the address. The taxi drops him off at the alley that runs behind Bradford Real Estate Holdings. Bob walks until he gets to the dumpster. Billy is standing by it, looking tall and clean as before.

"I am your determined protector," Billy proclaims in his usual greeting, smiling.

"Billy, you look great!" Bob says, then quickly continues, "What do you have in the cart?"

"Let's start with the hat," Billy chuckles. His smile is confident. He pulls out an old, tattered, black cap and puts it on Bob's head. He is looking directly at Bob, studying him closely.

"I've never seen hair that color or skin. There's so much I do not know about you. The way you walk, the accent, the way you look at everything." He shrugs. "Anyway, the hat will take care of the hair. Step behind the dumpster. I'll hand you my old shirt and jeans."

Bob changes into Billy's old jean jacket and steps out from behind the dumpster. "Well, what do you think?"

"Your walk," Billy notes, "Your walk is too easy. You need to look tired and defeated. You walk like you are floating. Slump your shoulders some. Try it." Billy crosses his arms, taking the pose of a judge.

Bob takes a few steps.

"You don't look defeated enough. More slumping. Try again."

Bob stops, slumps his shoulders further, stoops more, and starts walking again.

"Slower."

Bob slows down.

"Yes, now you have it! Now try to look grim. You're hiding, so never make eye contact."

"Thanks, Billy."

Billy nods. "Why are you hiding?"

"They think I have a power they can use," Bob replies.

"They?"

"Weapons people," Bob clarifies.

Billy frowns. "What did you do?"

"We helped."

"We?" Billy asks, beyond puzzled.

"It is complicated," Bob sighs. "If this works, you will know. Everyone will know."

"What's going to happen? Is your mission completed?"

"No. There is a chance, a good chance things could change."

"Change? When?"

"Soon, soon, " Bob says, "Until then, I cannot be found or recognized. I cannot return to my apartment. Any ideas?"

Billy thinks for a moment. "The homeless shelter. You could stay there. No weapons people there."

"Perfect." Bob pauses. "Cameras, are we going to pass any cameras on our way?"

Billy nods. "Yes, there's one on a crosswalk. The disguise is good, though; keep the cart in front of you, remember the walk, and you'll be fine. The two of us can walk together. It'll give you some practice with the disguise."

"You have talked me into it. Lead on determined protector."

As they walk, Bob makes a call on his phone. "Don, Billy will keep me concealed until morning." Bob listens for a few moments. "Of course, we will see what morning brings."

"Who *is* Don?" Billy asks quietly.

"A helper."

"Does he know what you did?"

"Yes. He was there."

They walk out of the alley, Bob pushing the grocery cart. It looks like they've switched ways of living, with Billy clean-shaven and Bob in ragged clothes.

"You look terrific," Bob says again. "There is a difference about you."

Billy smiles. "I went to the shelter. They needed someone to help, so I got the job. So, do you need anything from your apartment?"

"No. I have my camera in my bag. Nothing there that I need."

They reach the shelter; a sign above the door says, "Welcome." Inside is a large room filled with tables and chairs. At the rear of the room is a long serving counter with plates at one end.

"Let me show you my room." They pass through the dining area and kitchen. Bob opens the door to reveal a single bed, dresser, small table and couch. "You can have the bed or couch," Billy offers. "Hungry? There may be some leftovers."

"Yes. I had a light supper with Grace and Jack, but after what happened I could use something."

Billy leaves but returns shortly with a plate of mac and cheese. He hands it to Bob. "I warmed it up in the microwave."

Bob takes a big spoonful, eating quickly, "Thank you, Billy."

"How long do you need to hide?"

"Probably just tonight."

"You said things could change," Billy asks, "Has it begun?"

"I will know by morning. That is all I can tell you for now."

Bob puts the empty plate on the table, returns to the couch, and lies down.

"I have questions," Billy says, but Bob cuts him off.

"Tomorrow, there may be answers." Bob closes his eyes.

They are both soon asleep. Bobs eye lids move rapidly. *The truck coming at them, his arms around Grace and Jack, the light.*

Bob smiles in his sleep and mutters out loud, "So glad we were there."

The smile stops as Bob's phone rings. The screen reads four a.m.; text moves across the screen. "Video leaked, find mother and son, hide. Team has completed communication breach."

Bob rises from the couch. "It has begun." He looks at Billy.

Billy shakes his head. "So many questions."

"Turn your phone on and watch the news!" Bob shouts, then rushes out of the building.

— 21 —

Run, Jack, Run

Grace lays in bed for a long time before she finally drops off to sleep.

She sees the truck coming at them in slow motion, the tires rolling over the curb, Bob's arm around her.

"So warm," she murmurs out loud.

The truck rolls closer, her eyes wide as she screams. Then the light, the hum, the truck stops. Bob releases her, reaches and lays his hand on her face, his fingers moving slowly down her face.

"More than a touch, more than a touch."

Her phone rings. She jolts awake and reaches over to grab the phone. The time on the screen says 4:10 a.m. Bob's name flashes on display.

She swipes to answer. "Hello, Bob."

"Good morning. You must meet me at Sam's as soon as you can." Bob's voice sounds like he is running.

"What? What do you mean, 'must?'"

"Must is a word we seldom use, but today, you *must*," he repeats.

Grace sits up quickly. "Why? A truck almost killed us. Somehow, you saved us, then you disappeared. We have questions! Who are you ?How did you...?"

Her voice is loud, but Bob's response is calm.

"Grace, do you remember what I said about a camera on the truck? I was right. The event was filmed. Someone put it on your internet. Powerful people will be looking for us. Meet me at Sam's as soon as you can. Hurry, they will be watching your house soon. And Grace, do *not* bring your phone; they will be tracking it!"

That final sentence makes her stomach turn, thinking about strangers harassing her and Jack. She rolls out of bed and hurries down the hallway to Jack's room. She walks to Jack's bed and touches his shoulder, waking him as gently as she can.

"Jack, we have to leave now. Hurry." Her voice was just above a whisper.

Jack grunts and mumbles, "What's going on?"

"Bob called. He said the...' event' from yesterday was filmed, and that people will be looking for us. We're supposed to meet him at Sam's as soon as possible. Get up and get dressed. Hurry!"

Grace runs back to her closet, grabs a blouse, and buttons it up. For a few seconds, she looks at her face in the mirror and stops, the image of the light around them and the hum echoing in her mind. Then, she grabs a wet washcloth and wipes her face, rubbing to remove the makeup. She runs her hand down the buttons of her shirt and grabs an NYC hat, tucking her blonde hair under it, the ponytail hanging out the back.

"Jack, are you ready? Wear a different T-shirt and put on a ball cap."

They are out the door in five minutes.

"Wow, we did that quickly," Jack says. "You must really think someone is looking for us."

"Yes, now walk faster!" Grace says. Jack tries his best to keep up with her.

"Mom, the feeling...What do you think?" Jack asks.

Grace shakes her head. "All I know right now is that Bob saved us."

"Yes, yes, he did. Somehow...somehow, I think Bob and the 'others' he mentioned were connected to something. Bob wasn't alone."

"You're quite the scientist," Grace says with a faint smile, "Good to have that part of you back."

"I'm trying to look at the facts. The feeling when it happened...I can't explain. Can you?"

"No, Jack, no I cannot," Grace answers, puffing a bit from the fast pace.

"The power...the governments will want the power, the light, and Bob!" Jack shouts.

Grace nods, "Yes, and us. Please keep your voice down."

They walk faster. Grace looks ahead to the sidewalk crossing and sees a black SUV stopped at the stoplight.

She grabs Jack and pulls him to a porch stoop next to the apartment building, "Get down." They sit down, their backs to the wall of the building. Grace's side is up against the porch stoop; she holds Jack close to her.

They watch four dark SUVs roll down the street toward their apartment building. When they stop, people get out and run into their building.

When they're all inside, Grace stands up.

"Run, Jack, run!"

— 22 —

Driving to the Light

The alarm's insistent beep, beep, beep stops as a hand grabs the phone. The screen says four a.m.

John De Falco rolls out of bed and dresses quickly. He walks to the bathroom, turns on the light, brushes his teeth, shaves, and runs a brush through his hair. He looks in the mirror. Dark eyebrows, the Italian genes evident. He looked like Jack, handsome. He pulls on a pair of jeans and a sweatshirt.

He walks to the kitchen, the coffee already made. He fills a travel mug and heads out the door. The small car sits in the driveway. He slips in behind the wheel and pushes a button. The GPS screen in the dash lights up. He taps some buttons on the screen. His voice gives instructions.

"Destination, White Plains, NY, 9805 Mill."

"Destination, White Plaines, 9805 Mill, 189 minutes." He pushes a few more buttons.

The car backs out of the driveway the screen changes, "Arrival now will be 7:39 a.m." He makes his way to the I-95 and merges in with the traffic, settling in for the drive. A large pack of cars and trucks move on the six lanes of traffic. John's voice instructs the vehicle. "Auto on." He lets go of the wheel.

John rides in silence, his mind a din of thoughts: Grace, Jack, the light, and Bob Goeman. He sighs and sips some more coffee.

Talking to no one, "I wonder what today will bring." The audio in the car answers. "John, would you like the news?"

"Yes. Turn on news."

The screen changes on the dash; a woman announcer appears. "This video supposedly came from a delivery truck's camera. We are trying to determine if it is a hoax. See for yourself."

He leans close to the screen as the truck speeds towards Grace and Jack, the man with his arms around them, then the light and the truck stops. The man touched Grace's face, then looked at Jack and turned towards the camera. The video is repeated several times.

The announcer's face fills the screen. "We know there are other cameras at this location. We are trying to see if they show the same thing."

John grabs the steering wheel and says loudly, "auto off," and floors the accelerator.

— 23 —

Now We See You

Two pairs of tennis shoes try to fly on the sidewalk, "Faster, Jack, faster." Grace urges Jack. They sprint to Sam's and are there in a few minutes. Sam is just readying the Kiosk and sees them coming.

"Wow, Jack, Grace, I almost didn't recognize you. Why so early?" he asks with a smile.

"Bob asked us to meet him here," Grace says quickly, panting.

"Bob asked you?" he asks. "The coffee, I just started the coffee, too early for coffee."

"No, I said *must*."

They turn to see Bob dressed in Billy's old clothes. The grocery cart sits in front of him, Billy's old hat covers his white hair.

He looks at Grace and bows his head for a moment. The blouse buttoned, hair tucked in under her ball cap, no makeup, there she was. Grace. The new Grace. Their eyes lock, just like they did when the youth tried to steal the purse. Now, she stands tall, confident. Bob smiles at her and nods.

"Good morning, Grace, Jack, Sam. Sam, wait to open and do not turn on the lights yet."

"Why Bob, and why are you dressed like that?"

"You will see," Bob moves to the rear of the kiosk, away from the street side. "Come be with me. Stand with me."

They move to the rear of the kiosk. Bob stands in front of them.

"Watch my phone."

The three huddle and lean towards Bob's phone.

The screen lights up, the caption crawling on the bottom of their screens, "Man saves mother and child. Unknown force stops UPS truck."

The announcer quickly speaks. His voice is agitated and excited. "Sources confirm that a driver at UPS leaked this video, which got millions of views all over the world in just a few minutes. We believe the footage is real!"

On the screen, the crash plays out in slow motion. Bob's back is towards the camera when the light engulfs them. The truck hits the light and stops. Bob looks first at Grace, touching her face slowly, then looks at Jack. Then Bob looks at the truck for some time before he runs away.

The clip runs over and over again. The caption reads, "Who is this man?"

"Bob...Bob, who are you?" Sam's face turns to the screen, then back to them. His eyes are wide, and he shouts, "Grace, Jack, what happened? Are you alright? When was this?" He crosses himself, pulling out the crucifix from under his t-shirt, laying it on top, brushing it softly. "How did you do that? Are you...the Messiah?"

"No, Sam. I am not your Messiah. Soon you will see. " Bob says calmly as he points back at his phone, "Watch."

At that moment, all the screens in the world go dark, then flicker several times. Two teenagers in Sydney Australia had to stop texting. Soccer fans' World Cup game went away. Stock market tickers, NORAD's giant screen, Facebook, Twitter. Fingers punch screens in vain. The entire world has been hacked. Every screen blinks on, showing an elderly human face—smooth, old, and calm. Short white hair lays flat over cinnamon-colored skin, over a face with a thin angular nose and relaxed blue eyes. The face waits several seconds before speaking, the world listens to the silence, then hears:

"Hello, my brothers and sisters." In New York, the viewers hear this in English; in Beijing it's Mandarin.

"We saved a mother and child yesterday in North America. This is not the first time this has happened; we have saved individuals before by being at some chaotic event at the right time. This time, though, the event was filmed and seen by many.

"We are not what you call angels or what you call God. We are from a different part of this infinity, observing, and recording your actions. Do not be afraid." The person pauses.

"We found you what you would call a long, long time ago."

The screen changes. A picture of the Earth appears.

The voice returns, now softer, reverent. "Look. *Look.* A little blue dot, hanging in the darkness. Just the right distance from a star, turning at just the right speed, orbiting around this star. A miracle. Watch my people, after they had come so far, so long ago, find your beginning.

The screen changes again and shows a small craft descending to Earth, round and glowing, a vast mothership. A perfect sphere. The craft hovers and lands at the ocean shore. Small drones emerge from the top as a door opens, and a tall, feminine figure walks gracefully down the ramp. A group of men and women follow her out of the vessel. The small drones hover above, behind, and in front of them, lights blinking, recording all.

The group walks to the waves and stops as the waves march onto their feet. They look down and watch the wetness cover their toes, ankles, legs, and higher. They jump slightly as the water touches their upper thighs and groin, then smile and laugh.

The water stretches to the horizon with no land in sight. The people are silent, holding their arms up to the blue sky in praise.

The first tall, graceful woman leans over, cups her hand, and scoops up a handful of the wonder, watching it drip through her fingers. She looks at each drop like it is a miracle.

She takes both hands and forms a cup, raising it close to her eyes.

Her facial expression changes to curiosity as she takes a round tube out of a case she carries and fills it with blue water. She holds it at eye level, looking at the lights on the side of the tube as they blink, then become constant.

The screen changes to show a cell dividing, then goes back to the woman's face, her eyes wide. She speaks a word once, twice, and then a third time. "Life," repeats over and over. Tears come out of the woman's eyes.

"Yes, we witnessed your beginning," the original narrator returns. "As my ancestors left, they wondered what would come out of this water, *your* water. Would it be like us? Would it be different from us? They left, knowing some of us would return someday to see what had come out of this miracle.

"So, we have returned."

The screen changes again, for a few seconds, showing thousands of long, round cylinders surrounded by small, indistinguishable objects, falling through clouds and rain into a stormy sea.

"When we entered your birthplace, immediately our data collection revealed your plight. Oxygen dropping, plankton decreasing. Your birthplace was now a depository for what you throw away. Nuclear weapons in your womb, the final insult.

"The chaos of your creation separated you. You evolved in different places: grassy plains, mountains, forests, deserts, and even ice. You explored and populated the globe. Billions of you cover this little blue dot."

Two hairs float suspended on the screen, turning in the air. The camera zooms in closer, closer, closer, until finally, cells, then twin helixes of DNA, turning slowly on the screen.

"Imagine our awe when we found this," the narrator continues. "One hair is from us, the other from you. Separated by so much time and unimaginable distances, yet there is no difference. The sequence is the same. Somehow, we are connected. How?

"In our world, there is one land mass. Geography was kind to us. We evolved together – one language, one skin tone. We, like you, were the only mammal that walked upright. We had a thumb and four fingers, and a powerful electric machine on top of our bodies, what you call a 'brain.'"

The narrator stops talking and holds up a hand, touching the thumb with each finger, looking with total concentration.

Then, looking directly at the viewer, "We, like you, learned what we could do with them. We picked up a rock and threw it – in our beginning, at each other. But we stopped throwing at each other long ago. One land mass meant no land to conquer, no cultures to change or eliminate. We had no wars. Our resources went to knowledge, learning, and exploration. While you were building weapons, we unraveled the mystery of quantum entanglement. We travel the universe."

He stops talking as if composing thoughts, then raises his head and looks straight into the camera, with eyes squinted and wrinkles on his forehead.

"You were divided from the start. Different languages, culture, race, religions. Now you have all these, weapons, division, and fear. You are killing others when their faith or even skin color is different. Even now, you are wondering what side we are on. There can be no sides!

"You are infantile. Nine billion of you on this blue dot, carrying your guns, afraid and alone. Your military weapons will cause your extinction, consuming to oblivion. You are killing your planet."

The screen changes again. A tall tower stands on the shore of an ocean. In the water are strange crafts.

"These towers will remove the carbon from your air. The crafts in the water will clean your oceans. We are giving you the plans for these devices, which run on fusion power. You will have to build thousands of these, *together*. These devices will only save your air and water – not humanity.

"We will contact you once more before we leave. We will give a gift, that, if used, will save you. You will see our craft soon; see how we have used our resources."

The screen goes dark.

The newscaster comes back on the screen in shock. "This…was seen all over the world. We…we don't know the source."

The three look, put their phones away and look at Bob in silence. Jack has a huge smile, Grace's eyes are soft and wide. Sam, mumbles, "I knew, I knew there was something about you."

Bob looks back at them. "Such small grains of white sugar, you call it. So good, so sweet. Such an interesting word, 'sweet.'" He sighs. "I will miss the sugar, and I will miss coffee, the pigeons flying, the city, sunrise, all the people walking to the Metro. All this life and you. You are not a taste, yet you are sweet and good. In front of the truck, with the universe all around us, we were one."

The other three watch him closely now, like they are looking at him for the first time.

"Yes, I will miss you. Jack, with your questions. Grace, your love for your son, your determination that his differences will not hinder him. Sam, your smile for every-one, more genuine than most in this place because of the suffering you have seen. And, of course, your coffee, with four sugars."

"You saved us," Grace whispers. Her face filled with emotion. "You just happened to be with us at the right time. Such power...how did you...?" Grace's hands reach out toward him.

"That light...Bob, how does it have power? What was that sound, the note?" Jack asks.

"Jack, Grace, you have questions. I will answer some of them." Bob takes a breath. "What do we want? We are here observing. There is nothing to be afraid of. We wanted to see what had happened here after millions of years. We wanted to see what had come out of the water."

"Who are you? Are you like us? You look like us. I mean, parts of you are different, but you are like us," Jack asks.

"Yes, Jack. We are just older. Ancient, compared to you, your world. As our leader said, we came back to see what happened. Would you be like us? We had to know. Would there be another miracle?"

"So, how did you do that light?" Grace leans towards him as she speaks.

"Your people will have that power if you can survive long enough. Now, of course, you would try to use it against each other, and because of it, the three of us need to disap-pear. They will be looking for us."

"Of course, you're right," Grace says. "Every major power is looking for you right now. They see that light as a new weapon, an advantage." Grace looks at Bob. "I know, more than most people, that it's true."

Bob's phone chimes. He looks down at the screen. "Time to go. Sam, I will not see you again. You will have to hire more help when people learn of us. Smile at them as you have me."

"I will, Bob." Sam crosses himself.

The three walk down the street to where the delivery van sits. Don is standing by it, wearing a Kippah.

"Good morning, Grace and Jack De Falco." He nods, then turns. "Bob, what do you think of my Kippah?"

"Nice. Fits you well," Bob says, then adds, "This is my associate, Don Wells."

"Good morning."

The side door of the van opens, and they all slip into the back. Don gets in to drive, and the van accelerates rapidly from the curb.

Jack looks at Don, looking at his skin color. "No one would know. No one would know you were here among us, watching us."

"Bob tells me you are an intelligent young man," Don says casually.

Instead of replying, Jack fires questions to Bob at rapid speed. "What is the gift? How will you give it? What would it do? Is it the bracelet?"

"I cannot tell you that yet. Some of those questions I can answer, but not now," Bob says.

"There were people looking for us this morning," Grace interjects, "And I'm pretty sure they were American. Are we safe?"

"We can protect you; we do not want to be found," Bob reassures her. "We are going to a place that will be relatively safe. The van is new; there is no film of it. How far are we Don?"

"Fifteen minutes away, and it is still early. five-thirty a.m. Eastern Standard Time."

"You used the word *relatively* safe."

"Grace, you know that there is no place on this planet that is truly safe."

The van is quiet as it makes its way through the early morning traffic.

— 24 —

Making Up

Far away from the van, a phone rings on a table in front of a couch. The screen shows 4:10 a.m.

"Dane Corrigan, Chief of Staff."

The man lying on the couch reaches for the phone. He sits up as he speaks. "Yes, good morning, Dane." He rubs his eyes and listens for some time, then sits up more sharply. "Repeat what you just said. Hang on, let me put this on speaker phone so I can get dressed."

"Mr. President, there's a video up on the internet that shows a man stopping a UPS truck with…with just a light of some kind. He saved a woman and her son. Sir, we believe this is real. There was a camera on the truck, someone leaked it."

"Hold on, I'm on my way. I'll be there in just a moment."

He grabs clothes off the back of a chair, quickly finishes dressing, and heads through some hallways to an elevator. Others are already there.

"Good morning, Mr. President," one woman says nervously.

"Good morning. Have you all watched it?"

They nod.

"Angus, you know all there is to know about technology. Is there any way it could be a prank?"

A young man dressed in a wrinkled white shirt, with an unshaven face and his red hair uncombed, looks at the President. "Could someone create that video and put it up on the internet? Yes. However, we have real-time film from *five other cameras* along the street that all show the same thing." He stops, getting his breath excited. "This video is real."

"Thank you, Angus."

They exit the elevator and walk into the briefing room. At the front is a large screen.

Everyone takes a seat. The President nods, and the video starts.

The video plays out again. Several different angles are shown from other cameras up and down the street; they all show the same thing. The man with his arms around the mother and child. The light. Him touching her face, turning, looking at the camera. Running away.

No one speaks.

Then the President stands up. "Do we know anything?" He says as he walks up to the screen.

A woman stands.

"Yes, Ann, what do you have?"

"Mr. President, the FBI has confirmed his name is Bob Goeman, supposed to be a freelance photographer," she says, reading from a tablet. "We have his address under surveillance. The woman is Grace De Falco and the kid is her son, Jack. She works at Parabola Systems as an engineer. She has access to sensitive data. There's no sign of them at their current address."

"Thank you, Ann," the President says with a nod, then turns to the others. "What do we know about the light, the power?"

"At this point, nothing," a man says, "But if you look closely, you can see that he touches his bracelet as he turns. We don't know what that means, but we're fairly certain it's important."

The television screen then goes dark, and flickers brightly several times. Then, an elderly human face.

"Mr. President, we've been hacked!" Angus says in astonishment, looking at his tablet. He punches at his screen in vain, then pulls out his phone, to much the same result. Everyone in the room checks their various devices, showing Angus as they do so. "It appears that...that *everyone* has been hacked," he says, incredulous.

The face speaks. "Hello my brothers and sisters."

Silence fills the room as the screen plays the rest of the footage. When the video stops, the room is silent.

"Angus...what happened?" The President says.

"They...they had the technology to hack *all* broadcast platforms *everywhere* in the world. Every screen. Every device, screen, every phone in the world. We were *all* seeing and hearing the same thing at the same time. In China, the voice is Mandrin; here it's English! How?"

The President goes to the front of the room, to the screen, looking at the face. Then he turns to look at the assembly. "I see a human being. What does everyone else see?"

There are nods of agreement in the room.

The President turns to Angus. "Angus, this was recorded, right?" When Angus nods, he continues, "Go back to the woman with her hands cupped, holding the water. Freeze the video when she speaks."

Angus taps a few buttons. The video moves to the woman holding the water.

"Can you zoom in on her eyes?" the President asks.

The frame changes. A close-up of the woman's face shows a tear rolling down her cheek.

"She is giving praise." The President says softly. He stops looking, running his hand through his hair and walks back to his chair to sit down. "The world has changed. Everything." Straightening again, he asks, "Ideas? Thoughts? What do we know?"

The FBI director raises her hand.

"Yes, Marge?"

"We need to find the woman and son. They could tell us more. And the man, Bob Goeman, of course," says Marge. "With those kinds of powers, he'll be hard to find, and of course, everyone will be looking for them."

"Thank you, Marge." To Angus, he says, "Go back to the video of the truck. Run it in slow motion. Be ready to stop it."

The truck jumps the curb crawling towards the three. Bob's arm goes around Jack, then Grace. Their faces appear over his arms, eyes wide and afraid before the truck stops. Bob looks at Jack, then reaches for Grace's face.

"Stop! Now run it in slow motion."

The open palm reaches and meets Grace's face.

"He did this out of love," the President says, "compassion." He points his finger at the image. "What a story those two must have."

"What are the instructions if we find them?" Ann asks.

The President doesn't respond. Instead, he says, "Run that part again, about a gift."

The video moves to the clip, "We will give a gift that, if used, will save you."

The President nods, then speaks to the room. "I want to address the nation this morning at 8 a.m. Eastern. By then, all the media outlets will have run the video." He turns to his staff writer. "Phyllis, I'm going to need a very brief statement. These will be the most important words you write for me. When we are finished here, walk with me, and I will give you some ideas."

"Yes, Mr. President."

"What do you want the FBI and law enforcement to do?" Marge asks.

"Nothing," the President replies. "I repeat, *nothing*. These people have come back to see us. If they want to talk to us, we'll let them. We wait."

"Mr. President..." A man speaks up.

"Yes, Dane?"

"I think we should put our military on alert. Look for these devices in the oceans, and when he touches the bracelet...it must have tremendous power."

The President snaps at Dane, "We started with rocks and spears, and now we're changing warheads to kill more people. Are any of us proud of that? Let's try something else for a change. Here are my orders: do *nothing* that treats these people as an enemy. That man stopped a *truck* with *light*! They travel the *universe*! We must communicate with these people. We won't go looking for him, the mother, her son, or these devices."

He stops, out of breath from shouting. Then his voice drops. "Are we clear on that? Absolutely clear?"

"Yes, Mr. President," the room mumbles before someone asks, "Any further orders?"

"Do not look for this man, or the woman and boy," the President repeats. "Do not move a single piece of military equipment without my approval. He said their craft will appear soon. I don't want a testosterone-driven jock reacting. The United States military is to *stand down*. Do not move even one goddamn gun!" He glares at the room, red-faced, and watches them cower.

"Yes, Mr. President."

The President exits the room with Phyllis walking beside him. Her constant companion, a phone, is in her hand, recording.

"Mr. President, I just want to say, well..." Phyllis says, tucking a greying hair away, "You know I have never been a major fan of the generals."

"Yes, I know, you're a die-hard liberal," the President says. He sighs, then says, "Phyllis, what I see is a reverence for life. Tears, hands held high, then this power used to save. And my God, they are *one*. One; what can we learn from them? What did you see?"

"It was like...like they were praying, in total reverence of finding us. He said they weren't deities. The light, though...we could see as spiritual; how could light have power?" She pauses. "And they say they're like us. Does that mean we could become like them if we survive long enough?"

"Can we survive long enough is the question," the President says. His face is sad and solemn.

"The 'afraid and alone' is dark but truthful," Phyllis says carefully. "Mr. President, the world has changed. We have to recognize that fact. I mean, we're children compared to them. He talked like we are children. And they've challenged everything about us."

"Yes, yes, your are right." the President agrees. "I want to try and calm the people. Recognize we're in trouble. This action of saving the mother and child is important. They used their power to save. They see the truth about us. I agree with these visitors that we are alone and afraid."

"I'm on it, Mr. President."

The President stops walking, turns around and sees Angus a short distance behind them. "Angus, I need you today. I'm going to my office to watch all this again. Meet me at the media room at 7:30."

"You got it, Mr. President."

The President looks at Angus and Phyllis, glances down at the floor, his eyes shut for an instant. "Angus, Phyllis...from now on, call me Craig or Mr. Cruz. The titles need to go. They don't feel right anymore. That is an order." With that, he walks away.

As he's walking, his phone chimes again, and he looks down at it.

A text message reads, "We need to talk. Please. The kids and I are going to make pancakes. 7 a.m. breakfast?"

He hits a button, preferring to talk.

"Morning, honey. Yes, I'll be there at seven." He listens briefly. "Yes, I've watched it all." He hangs up puts his phone in his pocket, then steps into the oval office, picks up a small device on his desk, and speaks into it.

"Play video from this morning's briefing." The screen on the side of the room comes on, showing the truck, Grace, Jack, and the man holding them. The old serene calm face, saying, "Hello, my brothers and sisters."

He continues to watch.

"We will give you a gift that, if used, will save you."

He hits the refresh button again and again.

"We will give you a gift that, if used, will save you."

He turns off the screen and sits in silence for some time. His voice muttering, again and again. "What is the gift? How did you become who you are?"

He stands up and walks out of the room, making his way to the family living quarters.

Carla sits in front of the television, watching the truck stop as it hits the light. Her eyes are bright and moist; there is a tissue in her hand. "My God, Craig, look at that. *Look* at that light. Who *is* he?"

"The world's changed," Craig agrees. "What is their gift? Could it save us?"

Carla turns to him. "About last night. I overreacted, but...chemical warfare. Jesus, I never thought it would come to that. I'm sorry."

"I understand," he says, sinking onto the couch beside her, "Neither did I. The climate, the crops. People are starving. What's going to happen? I'm supposed to have all this power, but I feel so powerless."

At that moment, two children come running into the room and jump on the couch. The girl crawls up in her dad's lap. He strokes her hair. "Oh, I needed you, and here you are. Hi, sweetie."

The boy crawls up into Carla's lap. She takes a breath and smiles.

The four of them sit there in the quiet for a few moments.

"We're getting ready to have pancakes," the little girl says. "Daddy, can you stay long enough to eat? I helped make them. Please." She looks up at him.

"I helped too! Stay, Daddy, stay," the boy says.

"Craig, they've not seen you for two days. And they made some amazing pancakes. Wait till you see them," she laughs.

"Okay," Craig says with a sigh, "I guess I have time for a pancake."

The children cheer. They all walk to the kitchen and sit down at the table. Several misshapen, slightly burned pancakes sit on a white platter; Craig and Carla look at each other, smiling.

"They look delicious," Craig says.

The boy reaches across the table and grabs a pancake off the stack, and runs around to Craig's place at the table. He puts it on his dad's plate.

"This one is mine!" he says proudly.

The girl does precisely the same thing. "Mine is crispier. You'll know when you taste it." She hits the pancake repeatedly with her palm, smiling as she does.

"I'm sure they are equally wonderful," Craig says. He puts the syrup on the pancakes and takes a bite. He chews aggressively as the children watch him.

"How is it, Daddy?" the boy asks.

"These are the best pancakes I have ever had," Craig declares, and the children cheer again.

Carla chuckles. "So glad you could take time for this treat."

The family eats together, the children chattering about making the pancakes. After a while, the boy stops talking and looks at his dad more seriously.

"Dad, how come so many places are running out of food? Can't they just buy more?"

"Ah, Steve, my sensitive child," Craig sighs, "No, that's not the problem. Crops are failing around the world. It's sad that so many people are hungry."

There's silence around the table before the little girl says, "We can give them our pancakes."

Craig looks at Carla, putting his fork down. Their eyes lock: words not spoken fly between the two.

Then Craig gets up. "I need to go. It's already 7:30. I'm live in 30 minutes."

Carla stands up and walks him to the door. They embrace.

"Does this mean I'll sleep with you tonight?" he asks.

She smiles. "Go."

He walks to the media room and opens the door. Phyllis is waiting for him, ever-present yellow pad with her. There are several other people in the room, to run camera, sound, and lights. A large television is on one wall, a live news feed on the screen.

"One of my best few-liners, but I mean, look at the writing prompt!" Phyllis laughs nervously.

"What have you got for me?" asks Craig.

"It's brief, like you asked. At the most, three minutes. And it will, of course, be on the teleprompter," She hands him the pad. He scans it quickly and nods his head.

"We are ready, Mr. President. 7:45, fifteen minutes until we go live," a woman says.

Craig nods.

Then the screen in the front of the room changes.

High above the capital of the United States of America , there is an explosion of light, like bolts of lightning with no sound, a sky full of silent lighting. Out of nowhere comes a large, sphere-shaped craft.

The group in the room rushes to the balcony to look. Their heads tip back to see the craft, covered with dark scars and streaks on the gray, ancient surface.

Phyllis is the first to speak, her voice shaking "we're only children."

"Angus, where did it come from? How did it just appear? What do we know?!" Craig shouts.

Angus listens to his earbuds, shaking his head. "Out of…of *nowhere*. It's centered directly over us, the capital, 80 miles up. Circumference estimated at six hundred miles, about a tenth the size of our moon. We're looking at the largest machine ever made."

Suddenly the craft streaks away, a trail of light all that is left.

"Are they tracking it?" Craig asks.

Angus nods. He stops for a few seconds, listening to his ear bud. "Yes, yes." He shakes his head in disbelief. "It's now stationary over Moscow. In just a few minutes; how?"

Mr. President – uh, Craig, do you want to start before 8 am?" Phyllis asks.

"No. No, they're saying hello. Washington, D. C. then Moscow. Let the people watch this. It'll make them think."

"I.T. reported our computer network was hacked again. They didn't take anything, but they sent a download of technical data. The first page is titled, 'Fusion Power. Carbon removal from the atmosphere.'" Angus shakes his head again. "It's a huge amount of data. And we can't detect any propulsion power." He pauses, listening. "Just a minute, it moved again. It's now stationary over Beijing. It's dark there, but the city is bathed in light from the craft."

The group filters back into the room from the balcony. Craig takes a chair and looks at the camera. The clock on the wall says 7:59:50. He looks at Phyllis.

"I hope they're watching."

— 25 —

Showtime

The silence in the van is broken by Don. "I am hungry. We should stop at one of those 24-hour places and grab a few things."

"Food? You're thinking about food?! Where are we going? What are you doing here? Is there some kind of plan? What's going to happen to us?" Grace barks the questions at him and Bob.

"Yes, there is a plan," Bob replies, still calm.

"What are you people *doing* here?" Grace repeats.

"We have been studying you. Your world, your environment, and your military weapons," says Bob.

"How many of you are there?"

"Three-thousand."

"Three-thousand? Where are they?" Grace asks.

"Spread out all over the planet. Mostly along the coastlines of your oceans."

"What do you want?" Grace says again; the words come out sharp.

"Nothing, other than to learn how you evolved and changed."

"What about Jack, and me?" Her voice is strained, on edge.

"If our gift works, everything can change."

"What do you mean *if* the gift works?"

"You know the world has too many weapons. Your planet is sick. Our gift could change that. Right now, the world thinks we are a deity, a god, or the Messiah. The world thinks we can save them."

"Can you?" Jack asks, excitement in his voice.

"No, but the gift could."

"What the hell *is* the gift!" Grace shouts in frustration.

"You will see," Bob says, unphased. "Don, how close are we? You are right, we need some food. You could go in there with your new disguise."

"I will watch for somewhere to stop," replies Don. Soon, the van exits the freeway. He pulls over and parks. "Give me some suggestions, since this will be my first large grocery buying experience."

Grace sighs in defeat. "Okay, grab a pencil and paper. I'll give you a list."

"I will be okay," Don just smiles.

Grace starts rattling off items. Don listens patiently, merely nodding his head.

Jack starts to get out of the van, but Bob stops him. "Jack, you cannot go with Don. Look over there across the street. What do you see at the intersection? Look closely."

"Oh, I see the camera. Never mind, I'll stay here." Jack nestles back in.

"Yes, your world has them everywhere. So strange, all of you watching each other. Not talking to each other, only looking. Like you have become mute."

"Bob, would you please stop being so damn analytical and tell me what the hell is going to happen?!" Grace snaps, finally losing it. Her face strains, and her eyes water; she no longer looks confident, just frightened.

"I understand your concern for Jack," Bob says patiently. "But you need to remain calm. You have a chance to change things for this world."

This makes her stop and stare. "Me? How would I change any of this?"

"Grace, have the governments, the rich, the powerful, and your religions made this world better?"

"You ask tough questions." She pauses. "No. No, we're in trouble."

"More than trouble. Close to extinction."

"Extinction? What do you mean?" Jack asks, knee bouncing.

"Jack, things could change. There is an excellent chance."

"How, Bob?"

"You will see. We will show you."

"I need to call John, tell him we are safe. Will it be a safe call?" Grace asks.

"We can make it a safe call, use my phone. When you are done, I need to speak to your husband." Bob hands Grace his phone.

Grace takes the phone and dials a number. "John, we're safe. We're with Bob, and going to location where we'll be safe." Grace listens for a moment. "He wants to know where we are going; he's on his way."

Bob reaches for the phone, "John, I will text you the address. After you get that text, write the address down and turn your phone off. Buy a burner phone." Bob listens for a few moments.

"There will be answers, John." He stops the call, pushes some buttons on the phone sending the address.

"What did he ask you?"

"He said, 'I have infinite questions. Infinite.'

"Okay, got it all," Don says as he sets several sacks in the van.

"You remember everything, don't you? No list," Jack says.

"Yes, I do. I even got your favorite cereal. Chocolate Chex! I look forward to trying it. Chocolate Chex. What a name for food!" He laughs loudly.

"Why do you guys like food so much?" Jack asks.

Don simply replies, "We have missed it."

The van enters the traffic again. Eventually, they pull up in front of a garage in an industrial area. Don pushes buttons on his phone, and the garage door opens. The van pulls in, and the garage door behind them closes. Then the wall in front of the van slides aside, and the van pulls into another area. The wall closes behind them.

"Home sweet home," says Don.

They disembark.

"Just the basics," Bob says, "Some cots, a bathroom, and a stove for cooking. We will be safe here. It is a good place for us to tell our story." He opens his bag and takes out his camera and a small globe. It is the size of a small canta-loupe, gray, and metallic. "Jack, take this and go up those stairs. They lead to the roof. Put this up there."

"What is it?"

"Connection. A very good connection."

"You know I'm not that coordinated. What if I drop it?"

"You cannot break it. Do not worry."

Jack goes to the stairs and walks up, returning a few moments later.

Bob unfolds a collapsible tripod and puts his camera on it, positioning it in front of a table that has chairs around it. He takes out his phone and looks at it occasionally. Don points a remote at a very large monitor on the wall and it lights up with the weather station.

"Scientists today released data confirming that 90 percent of the methane gas from the Arctic Tundra has been released. Additionally, the prolonged drought in Russia is driving up the prices of grain. Canada is not selling their stocks of grain on the world market, citing that their country, 'may need it.'"

"More of the same news," Don says as he mutes the tv. He puts the groceries away in the kitchenette.

"What is the round thing on the roof for? You said connection?" Grace asks.

"That will let us talk to the world, just like when our leader did. Just call it a perfect antenna."

"Who are you going to be talking to?"

"Everyone. If this works, thousands of years from now, people will tell this story, of how a mother and son talked to the world! Not a leader, not a government, but a mother and son who told the world the truth."

"What do you mean? Mother and son talking to the world?" Grace says. Her voice shakes.

"You will see. You will see. There is a chance."

"I am empty. Let us eat. I have ingredients for sandwiches. I am starving!" Don announces.

"How can you talk of eating?" Grace groans quietly.

"Make your sandwich, Grace. We will sit, eat, and talk," Bob says.

They all take turns getting their sandwiches ready before sitting down at the table. Jack makes his food first; for some reason, he waits to start eating. Everyone sits down, looking at Jack.

"Jack, I know you are starving, yet you waited to partake. Is this usual?" Bob asks.

"No, no, it is not Bob. You said the word extinction. Not of some creature or plant, but of us." Jack looks at his mother, lip quivering. "I need to see my dad again soon."

"Yes, we both need to see him," Grace says.

Don ignores the conversation. He takes a big bite out of his sandwich, smiling, closing his eyes as he chews.

"You act as if you've never eaten before," Grace comments tiredly, looking at Don.

"It has been a long time since we have consumed," Don answers.

"What have you been doing in all of this?" Grace asks.

"I have been managing the collection of data from military and research facilities; you would call it spying," he says, still smiling.

"Where?"

"The United States of America and other places."

"What do you mean by other places?"

"The four other major military powers."

She stares. "What have you collected?"

Don chews and swallows. He looks at her intently. "The United States of America is changing their nuclear warheads to chemical. Others are doing the same thing. The food shortages have made them realize they cannot use nuclear weapons; they must have agriculture and infrastructure to produce food. The hypersonic missiles still have nukes. These of course are for destroying command, control, and leader's bunkers."

Jack puts down his sandwich. Grace just looks at Don.

"So...just kill the people? Move-in and produce food?" Jack asks.

"Yes, yes, Jack. The big boys' toys have changed. No longer will they be exploding thermonuclear weapons in the oceans, under the earth, or in the sky. Every building will remain standing. Even trees and grass will grow. Central Park would still be there. They are finally being truthful. The weapons are just for killing people."

"So...that's why they were changing the missile loads. This explains the glide path," Grace says slowly.

"Yes, Grace, you are correct."

"Oh, my God. What have I been doing?"

"Everyone thinks they are powerless. The person using a screwdriver to install a part on a missile thinks someone will just take their place if they quit their job. There is a chance—an excellent chance—that could change," Bob says, his voice getting louder as he talks.

"How?" Grace asks.

"You and Jack need to tell your story. Convince them we are just like you, only older."

"How are we going to save this?"

"The Messiah can be here now." Grace stares as Bob continues, "He, she, they are all of you."

"How?"

"All of you will have to decide not to go to war," says Bob. "No one can launch."

"If you know anything about us, you know those in power save their asses. It's easy to push a button when you are safe in a bunker!" Grace spits the last few words.

"This time, the entire world is going to know where those bunkers are," Don says.

She blinks. "How will they know?"

"Don, turn our screen on," Bob says. Don picks up a remote, smiling, as he pushes a button.

"Now you are all equal, so proud of the team," he says.

The screen shows a flat map of the world. On the oceans are many different colored dots. The land also shows several small dolls on the different countries of the world.

"The dots are the different countries' submarines. The dolls are each country's leader," explains Bob. "This is live data. We tagged every world leader and all submarines. The color code that indentifys each country is at the bottom of the screen. In a few moments, we will send this data to every email address and cell phone in the world. No more secrets. No one can hide."

"What do you mean, you tagged them?" Grace asks.

Don takes another bite, stares at her, chews, and swallows. "Some of you have used trace elements to kill people. We used it to tag food. Harmless of course." He takes another bite of his sandwich.

"This is crazy," Grace says, shaking her head, "Someone will launch immediately."

"Grace, the leaders just give the orders. Someone must follow them. By telling the entire world, we have a chance."

"It's too big of a risk! We'll all be killed!" Grace shouts. Silence fills the room.

Bob takes a big breath. He looks at them. "Your planet will die if you do not change. It is time to face reality."

"Is this all of your gift?" Grace's voice is soft again; she rubs her forehead.

"This, and the plans we have given you for devices that will clean your air and oceans. You have the technology to do it, but all countries must participate to be successful. It would start rebuilding your environment. Take away the reasons for going to war."

"How do you know these cleaning devices will do the job?" Grace asks.

"Because a long time ago, on our world, we had to use them. We were consuming to oblivion. Our environment became so toxic that we could not procreate; we became sterile. Without frozen eggs and sperm, we would have become extinct.

We had to confront who we were. You can change; we are the proof."

Grace looks at Jack. They stared at each other, trying to accept what Bob had just said. Finally, Jack speaks.

"The man on the screen said our DNA is the same. So…we can do this too. We can evolve. Someday…." Jacks voice trails off. "We could become like you are? We could travel, could go anywhere, do anything?"

"Yes, Jack, yes. Someday. We are the proof," Bob repeats.

"But the war...we wouldn't survive," Grace says.

"With the military data available here, there is a summation: no one can win. For the first time in the history of your world, all would know the war's outcome from its onset. The people should see there is no reason for ever launching. This, of course, is the last part of our leader's broadcast."

"It gives the world a chance. I could have a life," Jack says softly.

Don gets up from the table. He goes over to the food and comes back with four plates and the cake. He cuts and slides them in front of everyone. "Dessert. Turn the sound back on the television. It will give us an idea of how the world is reacting to us."

Jack grabs the remote and turns it on. The bottom of the screen reads, "President to speak at 8 a.m. eastern time."

Then the screen changes; there is a ship over Washington, D. C.

"There it is!" Don shouts, "Our home!"

The sphere fills the screen. Gray, dark streaks like burn marks cover some of the outside, all over the sphere. Curved lines and dots are visible on the surface.

"Oh my God. How big is it?" Grace asks as she marvels at the ancient machine.

"Big enough for all of us. Six hundred miles in diameter," Bob says, smiling.

"We have not seen it from this vantage point for so long. It is so beautiful!" Don says.

"600 miles!" Grace exclaims.

At that moment it streaks away.

"What is it doing?" Jack asks.

"First, it will make some quick stops. Then it will orbit the earth so that all on the planet see it," Don says.

"What do you mean quick stops?"

"Moscow, Beijing, New Delhi, Pyongyang, England, and more, we want complete attention. Then we will orbit the earth, so everyone sees us."

"This might just help," Grace says.

"What do you mean?" Jack asks.

"It, the ship, makes us look so small. So insignificant. Even a world leader with a huge ego must look at that and wonder how, who, why and what kind of power do they have? Surely, they are feeling awe...and I hope fear," Grace says.

"Okay, here we go," Bob says. He looks at Don as the president's face fills the screen.

"Good morning," the president begins.

"As we discovered just hours ago, our world changed yesterday. Beings like us, who looked in the waters of Earth, saw life, and raised their hands in praise have returned to see us. One of them chose to save a mother and child." He pauses for a long time. "You told us not to be afraid of you. Your actions prove that we shouldn't be."

He takes a deep breath. "You're right; we *are* alone, and we *are* afraid of each other. We have too many weapons and not enough food. We kill others over beliefs, petty differences, and even the color of their skin. None of us can prove what we worship, and yet sometimes we kill because someone believes differently than we do. You are right, we are infantile."

He pauses again.

"In many of our faiths, the concept of light is a spiritual one. You used it to help, to save a mother and her child. I see you as human like us; to say that I am in awe of you would be an understatement. What is possible? What could we learn from you? How did you become what you are? How can light stop a truck?

"To all of you watching, as you go about your day, as you look up and see their craft, *look*, and see the possibilities, their DNA is like ours. Think of what that means! They've already given us data so we can produce the once-unknowable power of fusion. Clean, unending energy. These people are here to help."

He stands up and walks close to the camera.

"We will not look for you, stranger, or the mother and son. We'll wait for you to contact us. To that mother and son...what a story you have. We all want to hear this."

He pauses for several seconds.

"Every President has closed their remarks to the nation the same way: 'God Bless.' Today, I say this:

"God Bless all of the people on this planet."

The screen returns to the announcer, and Bob turns off the tv with a smile.

"We got a break! Think of the timing. The President of the United States has just said he wants to hear our story. We did not even plan on anyone helping!" he says.

"The first world leader to admit that we have too many weapons...Suddenly I'm not as nervous!" Grace laughs in relief. Then she asks, "So, the leader is starting with the gifts?"

"Yes, he will start with the cleaning of the oceans and the air. The planet must be fixed, and all nations will have to build these devices together."

"You rehearsed this with your leader?" Grace asks.

"It will be okay," Bob says. "The last part will be the release of everyone's military secrets."

"I wonder what the world would be like if this worked," Jack says. His young eyes are bright in a way Grace hasn't seen in all his eleven years. "The world has never been able to vote on going to war."

Don is making adjustments to Bob's camera.

"We are ready. I will see if we are, as they say, ready for "showtime.""

A soap opera flickers off and goes blank as Don touches a button on his camera. He releases the button, and the sappy couple appears back on the screen, looking longingly at each other.

"Ready."

"Grace, Jack, have a seat at the table, please," says Bob.

Grace and Jack go over and sit down. Bob goes over and sits with them. Grace is rubbing her forehead; her knee is going up and down rapidly.

Bob sees her. "Grace?"

"Why me and Jack?"

"The world will believe you," he says simply. "You are not a leader, you have no power, you have nothing to gain. The two of you have something very special to share with the world."

"We're the only two people that have been...that have seen, or felt, or *know* what is possible," Jack says, his hands waving excitedly.

"Yes, Jack. Yes, you are. The world will believe you," Bob repeats.

"How are your nerves?" Don asks.

"Are we going to be talking to the entire world?" Jack asks.

"Yes, you are?"

"Ok." Jack thinks for a moment. "The light did something to me. I feel calmer than I probably should."

"Grace, how about you?"

"Overwhelmed," she says. "The world is hanging by a thread; what am I supposed to say?"

"The truth. That always works. You cannot say anything wrong or bad. I will lead you. This is not a contest. Just be authentic about yourself, me, and this world. You are a mother and a good one. Talk to those mothers and fathers that are wondering how they are going to survive, raise their children in this world." Bob turns and gestures. "Don, if you please."

The television screen flickers. Jack and Grace tense, looking at the camera. Bob moves to stand in front of it.

Bob's face appears on the screen. "Hello. As we have said, I am not a God, Messiah, or supernatural being. We are just like you, only older. We are one. You have nothing to fear.

"I have Grace and Jack De Falco with me. Grace, a mother, and Jack, a son. By now, all of you have seen the film of us in front of the truck. Grace and Jack represent no government or religion. They would like to talk to you and tell you about me and your earth, and," he stops for a few seconds holding up his hand, turning his bracelet slowly, "The light."

Bob sits down in a chair next to Jack and Grace.

"Would you please tell the world how we met?"

Grace hesitates.

"These are people just like you. You can be one with them," Bob reassures her.

She nods, then begins. "I was on my way to look at a school for my son, and a rat was running on the curb with a piece of pizza. Bob took pictures of it and talked like he had never seen one before. He said something like, 'Why would homo sapiens throw away food while so many of them are hungry?'

"Many of you watching this now would love a piece of pizza. One piece would be enough for two of you. Why would anyone throw food away? Bob went on to say that there were about thirty-nine million rats in New York City and only nine million humans. The rats survive on what we call our leftovers." She pauses, looking over at Bob.

"Jack, what do you remember about that day and the rat?" Bob asks.

Jack speaks quickly. "You showed me the pictures of the rat. I could tell by looking at her that she had been nursing her young. The rat, a mother, a mammal like us, had enough food so she could feed her young. Many of you have babies that are crying because of hunger. You noticed that she, the rat, had food."

Grace chimes back in. "At the time, I thought Bob was different, maybe disabled or something. He talked funny, using words we normally don't, had an unrecognizable accent, and walked like he was floating." She pauses. "Later that day, he stopped someone from stealing my purse by only using words. Now I realize he had powers I didn't understand."

"Grace, when I handed you your purse, can you tell everyone what you felt?"

She pauses again, then talks slowly. "A...calmness, that I had never experienced before. You looked...*into* me, not *at* me."

"Thank you, Grace. Jack, can you tell us about yourself?"

"I'm eleven," he begins, "and I love math, numbers, history, and interesting facts. I have ADHD and Aspergers, and other stuff, so Mom and the doctors say. People say I annoy them because I ask too many questions. I flick my wrist sometimes and bounce my knee, but...people tell me I have a nice smile." With that, Jack gives his smile.

Bob returns it. "How did we first meet, Jack?"

"We were at Sam's – which is a place to get coffee and donuts, on the sidewalk near our stop. You were there the morning after you stopped the man from stealing Mom's purse. We started riding the metro together. You walked to my school a few times. We were walking from there after a school program when the truck happened."

"Please tell us, Jack, what happened. I will run the film for you in slow motion."

The film of the truck plays in slow motion, as Jack describes it. "We were just getting to the corner of Main and Cicero. Then there was this sound, like a tire had blown out, and a crash. I looked, and a truck was heading for us, fast. You put one arm around me, one around Mom, and held us. I think I screamed; I was sure we'd die. Then…there was a light that surrounded us. A sound, too, a note? The truck hit the light and stopped."

"What did you see and feel in the light?"

"My Mom and Dad," Jack says, looking at the table. "We were all together. I could feel happiness. And it was like there were others with us, so many others. Like I was being held by them and a note I had never heard before. A kind of calmness."

"Calmness? Can you give us more detail, Jack?"

"All of my differences felt okay. Just DNA, just who I am. No sense in beating myself up about it. I felt like part of something much bigger."

Bob smiles at him. "Thank you, Jack. Another question. Can you tell the people why you think I am a Homo sapien like you?"

He thinks for a minute. "When you had your arm around me, it felt like you were my dad. And you love food, especially sugar."

Bob laughs. "Yes, I do love sugar. It is new to me. Thank you, Jack. What do you think is different about me?"

"You pay closer attention. You look closer. You see everything in detail as if you've never seen it before. Life, people walking to work, pigeons flying, sunlight hitting the skyscrapers, listening to me. You treat all of this like…" Jack stops collecting his thoughts, then says boldly, "Well, you treat it like it's a miracle."

"Thank you, Jack." Bob turns. "Grace. The light? Your memories?"

Grace wipes a tear before she says shakily, "The truck, the fear that Jack and I would be killed. The fear, then there were so many, so many of you holding us. Then saved! The awe, the scientist in me asking how, why, the rush of feelings. Jack's father and I were little kids. We were completely innocent and...well, perfect. I felt a connectedness to all, infinite."

"Where do you work?"

Grace fidgets awkwardly. "I work for the industrial-military complex. On weapons that would supposedly 'discourage' another country from attacking us."

"You use the word supposedly. Why?"

"Well...I just wonder where this is going to end. The constant spending on weapons when a third of the parents in the world are wondering how they'll feed their children. Hell, the rats here have more than some children."

"Grace, do you know why we are hiding?"

"Yes." She folds her arms close to herself. "Some people want the power that stopped the truck. They think that if they had you or us, they could have the power."

"Is that possible?"

She shakes her head. "No. I think I've realized what the light is."

"Grace, can you tell them what it is?"

She pauses. "It has nothing to do with power. You all are one. The light that wrapped around us was...all of you. This isn't a weapon; this is your form of love." Tears drop from her and Jack's eyes, but they are not openly crying; there are just tears and smiling.

"I think this is possible if we are one," Grace says.

"Everything has changed!" Jack shouts.

"Thank you, Grace and Jack De Falco."

The screen flickers, and the person with the elderly face appears. "We wanted this mother and son to tell their story. They have told you what is possible."

The screen changes.

"Here are images of your ocean eons ago. Clean, new, teeming with the start of life. The air and water were so clean you could eat the snow. Now breathe in a large city, and you choke. Your oceans' waves, once white with foam, float your trash. Your weather extremes now create crop shortages, and babies cry for food.

"Watch."

The screen shows a pile of drifting plastic containers on the surface of the ocean. In the distance, you see vessels moving in the waves of plastic and toxic waters.

"As mentioned, these vessels are robotic. In this simulation they are collecting the waste in your oceans. The tall cylinder coming out of the water would clean the pollutants from the water in your oceans. You will have to build millions of these and place them all over the world."

The camera angle moves to the shoreline and a tall tower.

"This device removes carbon from your atmosphere, turning it into building materials. These devices run on fusion power. Never-ending, non-polluting.

"You have built billions of automobiles and trucks. You have built massive warships that float on and in your oceans. Weapons that fly in the sky and space. You have split the atom. You can create these. You must stop building military weapons and build these together as one. That is the question, though: Can you be one?

"We are sending the data on how to build these, as well as our studies of the atmosphere and oceans, to all governments and universities of the world. Your planet must change to survive. This would stop the reasons for going to war. Yes, war. Watch."

The screen shows a series of images: a WWI soldier on a barbed wire fence, napalm on a running girl, a mother holding a scarred baby, people pawing through garbage,

Syria's chemical attack, and finally, the mushroom cloud over Hiroshima.

"These dead people never voted on the decision that killed them. Leaders of governments did. They were safe in their bunkers while you picked up your gun and marched to war, following orders. Believing your leaders were right. Parents saw their children go to war and never come home.

"I share this history before I tell you this: the five major military powers of the world are changing their nuclear warheads to chemical payloads. Nuclear would, of course, destroy your environment. Agriculture would be destroyed. The weapons are just for killing people."

The screen changes to a flat map of the planet.

"This is a live picture of the oceans of your world. You can see the colored dots on the oceans; they are the different countries' submarines. The color code at the bottom identifies each country. The miniature dolls you see on the screen on the land are the exact GPS location of every government leader. If there is a war, that leader will die with the rest of you. All your secrets are gone; you cannot hide any longer from each other. We are sending this data now to everyone. See and believe. Do not launch.

"Here you are—this miracle, out of the water. Alone and afraid. As one, you can be so much more. Goodbye."

The screen changes back to the announcer, who is silent, his face solemn.

At the bottom of the screen is a link labeled "NOSECRETS."

"There's...nothing on my teleprompter for me to say," he says sheepishly. "They've said it all. That's it, I guess."

A commercial plays, and the "NOSECRETS" link is still on the screen. Grace looks at her phone. On the screen is the same link.

"You, on your own, realized what our power is. There is nothing I would have added," Bob says.

"What do you think will happen now? Do you think someone will launch?" Jack asks.

"We hope that the world's leaders are talking to each other. I am sure they are all wondering how we got all their data and how we tagged them! They are probably all undressing, changing clothes." Don laughs.

"How can you laugh?" Grace says, frowning at Don, then at Bob. "You both seem so...*calm*. Someone could be thinking of launching a first strike right now; I am *so* scared. I want Jack to have a life, and I don't want to die. I have things to say to my husband."

"Grace, we have given the world the truth. You know that. For the first time in history. People of the world know what would happen if they went to war."

"Can we turn on the news?" Jack asks.

"Jack, we have given the leaders a lot to think about. Give them some time."

"Dessert," Don announces.

"Let us eat first," Bob says as he sits down. He picks up his fork and looks at Grace and Jack. "We may be leaving soon," Bob takes a bite.

"Had you already decided to release the data before the accident?" Grace asks.

"Yes. The way tensions have been building in the world, we did not know if there would be time to give you the gift. War was inevitable. Now we will see if the gift helps. We shall see," Bob says quietly.

There's a long pause before Grace asks, "Do you know the origin of all of this? How could we be the same?"

"No, we do not know. Think of the awe we felt when we came back and realized we were the same! Like us! How could that be?"

A horn outside stops the conversation.

"I believe John De Falco has arrived," Don says as he pushes the button. The door opens, and as the car pulls in, Bob says, "Don, let us go upstairs and look at the city." Don nods.

Jack gets up out of his chair and runs over to the car. The door swings open, and a tall, thin man with messy black hair and crooked, wire rim glasses steps out.

John pulls his son into a tight hug. He says nothing, just holding him. John's smile is enormous, like Jack's, as he rubs his back.

"Dad! We told the world the truth. Did you hear, did you, Dad?"

"Yes, I heard," says John. "You and your mother were amazing. I am *so* proud of you." He finally lets go of Jack and walks over to the table where Grace is sitting. "Hello, Grace."

"Hi, John."

"Why did they go upstairs?"

"They knew we needed to talk."

John turns to Jack, "Jack, can you go upstairs with your friends? Your Mom and I need to chat."

Jack nods and hustles up the stairs.

"Sit down, John," Grace says, gesturing toward the chair beside her. "If there is a launch, we won't have time to say anything."

John sits and leans toward her. He looks at her, the blouse buttoned all the way up and the lack of lipstick and mascara. Just her smooth face and blue eyes, blonde hair tucked in under her NYC hat.

"You look...different, and well...well," John stops. "I like the way you look."

"How sad I must've looked, staring in the mirror all the time. Wondering, 'Am I beautiful enough?'" She shrugs. "The answer was always no. Believing that my appearance, my sexuality was all I had to offer. How sad. I need to change."

John looks at the table and the wall. Anywhere but at Grace. "I always suspected something. But I didn't know what, and I was…afraid to confront you. Afraid it was me. Too scholarly, too quiet and afraid."

He stops, and turns towards her, "I need to change too. I know I have been opinionated about my faith. There are many ways to look at this, this miracle we find ourselves in."

Grace puts her hand on John's. "John, when Bob stopped the truck, I saw *us*. We were children, innocent and happy. I think we can be that."

Above them, Jack steps out onto the roof of the building and sees Don and Bob looking out over the city. Bob points at a flock of pigeons flying. They are both shaking their heads in disbelief.

He goes over and stands beside them. "So why the fascination with birds?"

"We did not have dinosaurs," Don laughs.

"So you've never seen birds?"

"Righ you are, Jack. They are amazing. Feathers, an airfoil," Don says.

"How soon will you be leaving?" Jack asks after a pause.

"We hope we will get to leave. If this works, we will leave at 9pm tonight," Bob replies.

"You mean you really don't know if this will work?" Jack asks.

"No. We are, as you say here, all in."

"What about the bracelet? You both have it on. Would it save you?"

"Jack, you see all. Yes, I touched it. We all have it. It connects us. But no, it would not save us," Don replies.

"If what we did today works, someday your people, in the future, could receive something like this at a certain age. A connection to all," Bob replies.

"Connection…Bob, can you call Lola on your phone? I know the number."

Bob dials the number.

Jack speaks into the phone. "Lola, it's Jack...Yes, I'm okay." He listens again. "It was wonderful. I'm different, and my differences are part of me. Some of them I can't change, and that's okay. Many of those differences are gifts." Silence. Jack listens. "We had to tell the truth. Things could change. The leaders will talk to each other." Listening. "Yes, I want to see you again too. I hope I get to. Bye, Lola."

Jack hands the phone back to Bob. "She said she likes me! Here I am, thinking I could die any minute, but I'm happy because Lola said she likes me."

Don and Bob look at each other.

Jack presses, "When you found us this time, did you know what you were going to try to do? Did you know we would be in trouble?"

"We knew your history. After we arrived, we became suspicious of all the weaponry changes," Bob says.

"If the truck hadn't come at us, would you still have released the data?"

"Yes. We had already decided to do that, but the crash helped. It helped show what is possible."

"Jack, look down there at the crosswalk," says Don. "Do you see the person getting ready to cross the street?

"Yes?"

"If they stepped out too quickly into the traffic and put their life in danger, would you stop them if you could?"

"Of course, I would...but I understand what you're saying. You're trying to stop us." He pauses. "I think we should go down now and turn on the TV."

Just as he says that Jack sees John and Grace come out of the door that leads onto the roof. They walk over to the three on the rooftop.

"Your son sees many things that others miss here. We will miss him," Bob says.

John walks up to Bob. He looks at him intently. Silence filled the air around them.

Then, he says, "Thank you for saving Grace and Jack."

"The equipment that just happened to be there was blocking the way. When the tire exploded, I knew where the truck would hit. Now you are here thanking me for being there. Here on this planet." Bob shakes his head. "Think all those little nanoseconds that put us here at this moment while this planet decides its future."

"I listened in the car," John says, "What do you think is going to happen?"

"Let us go down and turn on the television," Don replies.

They file down the stairs, Jack says, "My mouth is dry."

"Here we go," Don goes over and picks up the remote, turns, and looks at everyone.

The set flickers. Across the screen is a large caption.

"Satellites detect ground activity at launch sites in North Korea."

"No!" Jack screams. John and Grace reach for him, hugging tightly.

— 26 —

Decision Time

"North Korea! They only have a few missiles! What is Kim Jong-un thinking?" Don shouts, his face red with anger.

"He is an ego-driven man," spits Bob. "Or he has a weapon we do not know about. Don, we have team members there. Why haven't we heard from them? Call them now!" He turns to look at Grace, John, and Jack, hanging on to each other as Don's phone rings.

"What do you know?" Don bellows into the phone. He listens for just a few seconds. Yes, now do it."

"What?" Bob asks.

"The team members in Kalma are on their way to the Musdan-ri missile site; they want to breach communications, I said yes! They are seconds from the site!"

• • •

11pm. Kalma, North Korea.

A DHL delivery truck speeds down a narrow, bumpy gravel road. The headlights pierce the darkness as the engine screams along at eighty-five miles per hour. The truck tips and slides on the curves as the driver talks.

"Put it on the roof as soon as we pull up to the checkpoint," she says to her companion. Her hands grip the steering wheel tightly, a smooth grey bracelet is barely visible on her right wrist. She wears a DHL uniform, the ball cap covering most of her white hair and her thin angular, cinnamon face.

The passenger looks at her while hanging on as the truck hits another bump. Her bracelet moves on her wrist. The other hand holds a globe.

The truck hits a huge pothole and veers.

The passenger shouts back at her, "You got it. I see lights ahead. 10 seconds. We may be in time. I have it connected to the truck camera. Whatever happens, all will see."

The truck pulls up to a crowd of soldiers and military vehicles converged around a checkpoint. Cement barriers form a lane bordered with razor wire. Searchlights on poles make it bright as day.

The brakes squeak loudly as the tires slide to a stop in front of the crowd.

The soldiers point guns at each other; one man stands on the top of a truck and shouts something at the crowd. The soldiers turn as the truck pulls up in a cloud of dust, and those with guns point them at the truck.

The driver jumps out of the truck as the passenger puts the globe on top of it. They both toss their hats to the ground, short white hair now visible to all. The driver pushes a button on her phone and points it forward as both walk towards the crowd.

Everywhere in the world, screens display the two women striding, tall and confident, like giants, ignoring the rifles pointed at them.

"Hello everyone," says the driver in perfect Korean. "We are two of the visitors. We just arrived at the Musudan-ri missile site."

She turns her phone towards the crowd of soldiers. They stand like dogs told to sit, mute and following orders from their master.

The man on the roof of a truck jumps down and walks forward. He is thin, eyes sunken and lined with dark shadows and hollow cheeks. His uniform hangs on him as it would on a scarecrow.

His eyes focus on the two women's faces, marveling at their serene confidence with the rifles pointed at them. "You are...you are visitors? You are like Bob?"

His voice has a pleading sound to it as if to say, "please say 'yes.'"

"Yes, we are. Bob and the entire world can see and hear us now. What is happening here? Tell the world."

"Will everyone understand me? Everyone? Everywhere?"

"Yes. Everyone, everywhere, will understand you."

He nods his head, closes his eyes, and then starts to speak.

"I am Kim Syong." He stops, nervous. He breathes in deeply, and starts again, loudly. "I am only a soldier! I saw the broadcast. My commander told me to launch missiles, but...I did not follow the order to launch. Others joined me. There was a brief battle in the complex. We...we had to kill many of our countrymen to stop the launch. Central command sent more soldiers; their guns are pointed at us now. I've been trying to tell them what's possible. We're all starving."

The two women put an arm around the man's back, their hands joining. They look at each other, a slight nod. One says to the man, "Walk with us; be with us."

They stride towards the crowd of soldiers until they are in the crowd, faces inches from the guns still pointed at them. The first woman says, loudly, "You are starving, yet you have guns. You follow the orders of a leader who is fat while your children go to sleep hungry. How much rice could you buy with the cost of a gun?"

"We cannot launch!" Kim Syong shouts. "If we launch, there will be a counter strike and we will all be killed! We would be starting the end of the world."

A voice from the crowd shouts, "This is an American trick!"

"We are not Americans," says the woman. "We came to help you!"

With that, she touches her bracelet. The two women hold each other's hands tightly behind Kim Syongs back as the light surrounds them. They move closer to men with guns, the light slowly moving out around them until it engulfs the entire crowd. Then the humming starts, and it becomes a single note.

Eyes widen. There are gasps as guns fall to the ground. The light stops. There are murmurs, sighs, and words spoken softly. They all look at each other, then at the two women.

The two women look intently at the men. Then they close their eyes, hold their hands up to the sky, and tip their heads back. Their lips move.

They open their eyes and bow toward the crowd of soldiers.

"Mr. Syong, we are leaving. Thank you, Mr. Syong. You are more than just a soldier!"

"We just want to be able to feed our children," he says quietly. "Not too much to ask. Please, what are you called? What are your names?"

"Here, I am called Jackie," the tallest woman says.

"I am called Jaicee," the other replies.

Kim Syong, bows slightly, and says, "Angels."

"No, we are not angels. We are your sisters."

The woman turns the phone towards her face. Screens everywhere in the world see the tear running down her cheek as she says, "One man decided to not follow orders, and others joined him. The universe is singing."

An announcer's face appears on the screen. He stares. Finally, he speaks. "We may have a chance."

. . .

Don mutes the television as it goes to a commercial.

Bob, Jack, Don, Grace, and John all look at the screen in the garage, watching silently.

Finally, as the light stops, Jack speaks first. "How did they know they wouldn't be shot? They risked their lives for us."

"Yes, yes, they did. A wonderful team. Hope they find safety. They have revealed themselves," Bob says.

They all sit in silence for a long time, looking at each other.

Eventually, Bob pulls out his phone and makes a call. "Jackie? Jaicee? I am concerned. How are you going to conceal until we all depart?" He listens for some time, then breaks into a smile. "You made a friend, even a future leader. Tell him we are all so glad he was there." He pushes a button on his phone, nodding his head affirmatively as he says to the group, "Kim Syong's grandfather has a fishing shack on the coast of the sea. They will be safe there."

"Look, it says the White House is going to make an announcement," Grace says, pointing to the captioning on the screen.

"President to speak."

The Rose Garden at the White House appears, and the President comes out the door. He holds it open for his wife and children. The mother takes the hand of one child while the President takes the hand of the other.

They walk towards the cameras, the reporters waiting on the lawn.

The President clips the microphone to his lapel.

"Hello. We wanted to greet you all. This is the Cruz Family, Andrea, Steve, and Carla. We all send greetings to the world."

"As noted earlier this morning, we have been visited and studied by a much wiser, older, and united race of human beings. They are like us, with one remarkable difference." He pauses, looks down at his children, then to his wife, before returning to his speech. "The difference is they are one. They have an incredible power that they used to save a mother and child. Power to help a crowd of soldiers think for themselves. They are risking their lives for us." His voice breaking with emotion, eyes welling up. His wife looks at him, her lip quivering.

"Anything is possible, they have told us, if we are one as well. Think of it! Anything. They have given us tools that would enable us to save ourselves and this world. If we don't use these tools, we will destroy ourselves and this miracle.

"As such, I have recalled all our submarines. They will all be on the surface, moving at top speed to return to their families. All our military forces are standing down. The Cruz Family asks the rest of the world to do the same."

The family starts to turn and walk away, but the little girl jerks on her dad's hand. She looks up at him.

"What, Andrea?" he asks, baffled.

"Daddy, you forgot to tell them about the food!"

"Oh! Yes, I did." He looks back to the camera. "We are now loading our military transport planes with 10% of our grain stockpiles for select African countries and North Korea, who have both suffered the most with crop shortages.

We hope our transport planes are welcome because of the courageous actions of Kim Syong and his friends. I would welcome a phone call from Kim Syong; I want to thank him. I'll be talking to other leaders later this morning."

With that, he reaches down, picks up the girl, holds her close to him, and runs a hand over her hair. As he turns away from the camera, she whispers in his ear, and his microphone picks it up.

"Now they can make pancakes!"

He holds her closer. The family turns; the mother, holding the boy's hand, puts her other hand on her husband's shoulder. "Good job, Craig."

Grace mutes the television.

"Good for the President. He stepped up and started what we hope is a chain reaction. Clever to have his family with him outside."

"Look." Jack points at the television and waves his finger around.

Yang Li, the President of the Republic of China, is on screen, the translation beside him. He requests humanitarian aid; the southern parts of the country have suffered a disease in their rice crops. He has ordered his military to stand down as well, he explains. The submarines are on their way home. Yang Li bows to the cameras before going off-screen.

"China had the most missiles. Useless pride has disappeared. Good for him," Don says.

Another world leader appears.

"Russia will release 10% of their grain surplus."

"You, all of you, may have a chance. This could be a beginning," Don says. "It is up to the people. They must confront their governments, their leaders. We cannot do anything else."

"You're leaving now?" Grace asks.

"Yes," Bob says.

"What can I say? What question can I ask, knowing I will never see you again?" Jack says, voice thick with emotion.

"Be in awe of the miracles now, Jack. You, your mother, and your father are here now. Everyone we know goes somewhere else someday. Today they are here with you. Be in awe, even when sad."

Bob looks at Grace; their eyes lock. "Grace." He pauses, "Physicist, mathematician, analyst, mother, and mate. You are just beginning to look inward. When all of you do that, all, you will begin your journey to be truly one. Then it will be possible."

"How can I thank you for looking, really seeing me?"

"Pass it on."

She nods, "What about the bracelet?"

"Yes, it has amazing power and connects us all instantly. It took us millions of years. Use the gift we have given you. Then you will have millions of years. Keep telling them what is possible."

Bob bows slightly toward the three. Don joins him. They turn and walk to the van.

The family follows them silently, watching them get in and following it as it backs out of the garage into the street. They watch it roll down the street away from them.

John steps between Grace and Jack, puts his arms around their shoulders, pulling them close to him. Jack looks at his father, studying his face, then his mother.

"I am in awe to be here." Jack's booming voice fills the street.

— 27 —

Thank Who?

"Now what? Is everything going to be, okay?"

Jack turns to his parents, who can only shrug.

"We don't know if the governments will work together for longer than a day. The world now knows our governments have lied to us all. They almost killed all of us," John says in disbelief.

"Yes, they did," Jack agrees. "Yet that's not even the most important thing to happen today."

"What do you mean?" asks John as he looks down at his son.

"The definition of what's possible has changed."

Grace looks at her son, touches his shoulder, and smiles, saying nothing. John just shakes his head.

A car moves past them.

"We need to get out of the street," says Grace. "Someone could recognize us."

The three turn and go back into the garage. They sit down on the couch.

"Our lives won't be the same for a long time," Grace says.

"You're right. The media will be hounding us constantly. I don't know if I'll be able to return to the university," John replies.

"How am I going to go back to school? How am I going to see Lola?" Jack asks "I hadn't even thought of that. I was happy a minute ago, but...This is terrible!" He shudders.

"Come on, Jack, buck up. The world has a chance!" John doesn't try to hide his smile.

"But it's the truth! How are we going to live?" Jack's voice is tense.

"Maybe my boss could help. If the corporation builds these machines, if they change... I would have to call them and ask to speak to my boss—but what if they decide not to change and keep building weapons?" She stops, looking at John.

"Grace, it's a call worth the risk." John pulls out his phone and pushes some buttons.

"Found a number for Parabola Systems." He pushes the button on the phone and hands it to Grace.

Grace takes the phone; she rubs her forehead with her other hand. "Yes, Wayne Findley please."

Grace listens. "Yes, my name is Grace. He'll know which one."

Seconds tick by. Finally, "Hello Wayne."

She listens, occasionally nodding her head and looking at John. Then she says, "Let me put this on speaker so John and Jack can hear."

Wayne, apparently continuing a line of thought, says, "Relieved to hear from Grace! I have been worried and thinking about you. What I am suggesting is this: the world is looking for you, of course, but there is a nice apartment on the top floor of this building. Top military brass stays here while in town. They won't be staying here anymore, though. We're going to be building these devices that will start restoring the planet. Grace, with these power units, your other degree in physics is a good fit. We have security in the building; you'd be safe. What do you think?"

"I... would love to help," Grace says slowly, looking at John.

"Can Lola come to visit?" Jack interjects.

Wayne laughs. "Yes, Jack, you can have visitors."

"I would need transportation back to the college. Well, I don't know if they'll want me back there or not. Publicity and all," John says.

"John, we would be more than happy to help you in any way. We can offer a private car with a driver. And security, of course."

John nods at Grace and Jack.

"Wayne," says Grace with a smile, "John says yes!"

"Great! Send me your address or give me somewhere to meet you and I will be in the car. I cannot wait to hear this story!" With that, he hangs up the phone. Grace texts him the address.

"Well," says Grace, "looks like our new home is going to the top of the Parabola Systems building."

"The view from there will be fantastic! We will be able to see them!" Jack shouts.

"What do you mean?"

"Bob said we would see them leave; he said everybody would see them leave."

"What else did you talk about on the roof?" John asks.

"I used Bob's phone to call Lola. This was when we did not know if we were all going to die. She told me...she told me she liked me! I forgot about being scared. She likes me!"

"Did you tell her about what happened?" Grace asks.

"I told her it was wonderful. That I can use my differences to do good."

"You are absolutely right," John agrees.

"Oh, and I asked about their bracelets. Bob said someday, we could all have a device that connects us. And I know why they are fascinated with birds!"

"Why?" Grace asks.

"They never had dinosaurs! They had never seen birds before! Think of it. Seeing one for the first time! Airfoils, the wing…I had never thought about it!"

"You asked good questions, Jack," Grace laughs. "Did they say when they were going to leave?"

"Tonight, at nine. They must leave, I guess. They must, right? Everyone is looking for them. Of course, we are the only people who know how many there are— three thousand!"

"Three thousand?!" John repeats, amazed.

"Yes, mostly along the coastlines," Grace adds.

"Please tell me everything you remember about Bob," John says. Grace and Jack spend some time recounting their time with him. After a little while, John asks, "Grace, of all the memories you have of Bob, which one stands out the most?"

She remembers when he handed her the purse. The way he looked into her. "I think… it's that Bob focused on me not as an object, but as a person. Ignoring what I looked like. He looked at everything like it was a miracle, including me."

"I hope we can do that, the three of us. I know we're not as advanced, but we could try." Jack says. His voice has a pleading tone to it.

John looks at Grace, and she at him. Neither blink nor move.

Grace's phone chimes. She looks at it. "Wayne is here. John, can you open the door?"

John walks over and pushes the button, and the garage door opens. A long-stretch limo pulls in. The back door of the car opens.

"Hello, Grace! I told you we had to have hope," Wayne grins. He walks forward and extends his hand to John. "Wayne Findley."

"Good to meet you, Wayne. Thanks for the help with all of this. You know Grace, of course. This is Jack."

"Jack, your mother told me all about you. Now that the world knows you and your mother, I hope I can get to know you better. I have so many questions."

They get in the car, Wayne sits facing the rear. John, Grace, and Jack file into the seat facing the front. Wayne hits a button.

"Okay, Brock. We're ready, let's roll."

The limo backs out of the garage. A black SUV pulls out from the curb in front of them and one pulls up behind them.

Grace sees them. "Security?" she asks.

"Yes. There are some drones above us, too."

"This is quite the ride," says John.

"Yes, it is. Bulletproof. Used to transport people to the building where I work. Admirals, generals, colonels, presidents, princes, even kings. Pick a title that means power; it's been in this car. And today, it's carrying two people who may have changed the world."

He pauses, and leans forward towards Grace and Jack.

"Their only title? 'Mother and son.' Today, for the first time in a long time, I am excited about my job."

"We were only messengers. It was them, you know," Grace says.

"What is possible has changed forever! Forever!" Jack says.

"Jack, your mother, and I had lunch on her second day at work," says Wayne. "She talked about you. I can see why now."

"Jack has always been tuned into many things that people tend to miss," John says.

"John, I know you're an educator. What's your field?"

"I teach at Bingham University. Philosophy, and a course on the world's religions."

The car pulls into a basement parking area by an elevator. They exit the car, Wayne leads them to the elevator.

He talks as they ride up. "The apartment is completely furnished, but make a list of anything you need and we'll get it for you. Security can bring you food when you get settled. I'll send you a phone number. You'll be safe here."

The elevator stops on the 50th floor. The doors open, and the skyline of New York fills the windows.

"Wow!" Jack shouts, eyes wide as he looks around at the view.

"You haven't seen anything yet!" Wayne laughs. "Follow me." He walks over to a door, opens it, and walks up some steps. He opens a door and steps out onto the roof of the building, revealing a glass wall surrounding a swimming pool.

"Nothing but the best for the world's military," he jokes. "I'll let you get you settled in. Remember to make your list of what you need."

"Thank you so much," says John. "How can we repay you?"

"Professor De Falco, a gift opens the way and ushers the giver into the presence of the great."

"Ah, Proverbs," John nods. "Do you read the Bible, Wayne?"

"Sometimes," he replies. "I pick out the verses that make sense to me, and that one has always stuck with me, working here. I've kept thinking that someday, I could help. And here you are. So, welcome."

"You know, I just thought of something!" Jack cuts in.

"What would that be, Jack?" John asks.

"The rat with the pizza. We all need to thank her!"

The three adults look at Jack with their brows raised.

"As I said, Jack sees things that others miss," John explains and places his hand on his son's shoulder.

— 28 —

Going to Another Place

The van rolls through traffic. Finally, Don speaks. "I will miss Jack, the city, the cursing even. All this life. Look at them!"

"Yes, look at them," says Bob. "What will they do? Do you think they will change?"

"Yes, yes, I do. Think of what happened! Mothers and fathers did this. Not leaders or money. The President's wife was important. A *mother*. The man in North Korea and his friends, whose hearts hurt when their children cried from hunger. Mothers and fathers."

"Messiahs."

"Yes."

"I will miss Grace and Jack," Bob says quietly. "There are so many kinds of love."

"Yes."

The van rolls on, and the two are quiet. Finally, Bob speaks. "Go back to that IHOP. You know the one."

"Yes, the syrup. The waffles, our first coffee. I wonder if they serve waffles in the afternoon?"

"I hope so and the syrup. So much liquid sugar. The coffee and the sugar warmed you up."

"Yes, I was so cold, falling off my transport by the dock. The Atlantic Ocean is so cold. I was shivering. You were safe and dry on the dock, helping me out of the water. We walked in the darkness and found a sign. The aroma was wonderful. The woman came over, and I asked, 'Do you have a hot liquid that would raise my body temperature?'"

"I remember her looking at us, like something was wrong with us, shaking her head." Don laughs. "'Coffee, sit over there. What the hell happened to you?'"

Bob laughs, too. "When I told her you fell in, she said, 'No shit!' It was my first time hearing that word. So, I just sat down, and she brought us coffee. It was so bitter. I watched someone put the white crystals in their cup, so I tried it."

"Sugar. So good. We spent so long adding and tasting that she asked us whether we wanted to eat.. Of course, we had no idea what they had." Don chuckles.

"She suggested the waffle special."

"All you could eat for fifteen dollars!"

Bob laughs. "We ate them with nothing on them. She had her mouth open like we were strange or something."

Don laughs harder. "'What the fuck is wrong with you guys? Put some syrup on them.'"

"I used the blueberry. So sweet, so good. When I started driving, of course, I learned the word 'fuck' had multiple uses."

"I used maple," Don recalls. "Our last meal here. I want it to be memorable."

They pull up to the IHOP and are guided to a booth.

The server asks, "What can I get you today."

"Pot of coffee, please. Do you have the waffle special today?"

"Sure do! All you can eat, fifteen dollars each," she says with a grin.

"Fix us up with that. We would like blueberry and maple syrup, please," Bob tells her.

"You got it." She nods and walks away.

Bob leans towards Don. "I think we should use a boat. The Atlantic Ocean, as we learned, is very cold. The others can choose how they leave, but many will have much warmer water than we have."

"Using any kind of flotation device that would keep us out of the Atlantic Ocean is a clever idea."

"We have never been on top of the ocean before in the daylight. I would like to experience that. There is little wind today. The water should be calm." Bob pauses. "We want the last experience we have here to be memorable. We have at least six hours of daylight left. We have plenty of time to see some of the city skyline from the water."

Don pulls out his phone and types some, then laughs again. "I found a place where we can rent a boat. This will be easy. We can be like tourists!"

"Here you go, waffle specials, two of them, enjoy." The waitress places the plates down on the table. Bob takes the maple syrup off the syrup caddy and pours maple syrup on the waffle until submerged. The syrup is lapping on the sides of the dish. Don does the same with blueberry.

The waitress comes back over to refill the coffee cups and blinks at the plates. "Now that is some serious syrup!"

"So good, liquid sugar," Bob says.

He and Don stuff bites of waffles in their mouths, the syrup dripping off the forks, their faces filled with delight.

Don chews slowly, savoring the bite, then says, "I will miss it all."

They finish eating. Bob gets up first. "Save some of the cash for the boat rental tip. We should leave her a nice tip. Our last syrup."

"You got it." Don reaches into his billfold and puts a one-hundred-dollar bill under the plate.

Bob walks over to the waitress, "Thank you for the liquid sugar." The waitress looks at him, caught off guard by this strange remark. She watches them walk out, shaking her head some.

She goes over to the table, clears the plates, and sees the one-hundred-dollar bill. She stares at it, then at the door, unsure if it's real.

"A guy leaves me a one-hundred-dollar tip! Liquid sugar? Who are those guys?"

• • •

"There is the ocean, and the dock is right ahead."

Don points to the rent boat sign.

He pulls the van into a parking stall. "I learned to drive here. I will miss it. Strange. The illusion that the driver is in control. I will just leave the keys on the seat."

Bob takes out his phone and starts texting.

"What are you doing?" Don asks.

"I told our friends to be outside at nine p.m."

Don smiles and nods. "Yes. It will be nice to know they are watching."

They walk to the small cement block building. Don walks up to the counter to find an older man with an old t-shirt and a straw hat perched back on his head. The skin on his arms is brown and wrinkled from the sun.

He greets Don. "Good afternoon. What can I do for you?"

"It is a beautiful day; I wanted to rent a boat for a few hours. My friend takes a lot of pictures. Can we have it until sundown? What would you recommend? Something easy to operate. Quieter, the better."

The older man looks at them. "Well, if you are willing to pay, I have a new boat. Lithium battery, good for six
hours. You won't hear a thing except the water. It's one hundred dollars an hour. Big charge on your credit card until
you bring it back."

"How hard is it to operate?" Bob asks.

"Did you drive here?"

Don nods.

"Then you can do this boat. All you do is steer, a pedal
to go forward, a brake to stop or go backward. A kid could
do it." He walks them out to the boat. "If you get in trouble,
just push that red button there. It will blink for thirty seconds to let you prepare as it will return to the dock at extremely high speed, stopping exactly where it is now."

"It sounds like exactly what we are looking for."

They go back inside. Don pulls out his credit card and
hands it to the man.

"How many hours do you want. The battery is
good for six."

Don says, "What time is it?"

"3:40 by my phone."

"Five hours it is."

"The deposit on this baby is ten big ones. Refunded
back to your card when the boat is returned. No way you
can be late; the timer on the boat will kick in and bring
her back on time. There can't be any late charges with this
boat." The old man chuckles.

"What are late charges?" Don asks.

The old man looks at him strangely. "It's…a charge if
you had the boat for more hours than you paid for?"

"Got it. My first time renting a boat. This will be a
pleasant experience," Don nods.

The man hands Don his card. They walk towards the
dock. Bob brings up the rear, following Don, and they go
down some steps to the boat again.

"Go ahead and get in," the old man says and points to a compartment under one of the seats. "Life jackets, of course."

Don gets in first and goes to the seat where there is a steering wheel. Bob sits at the front with his bag by the chair. They both put on their life jackets.

"Okay, down at your right foot is a gas pedal, just like in a car. The other pedal is the brake. Of course, you are in the water, so it won't just stop." The man grins and chuckles. "You'll get the hang of it." He takes out his phone and dials a number. The dash in front of the steering wheel lights up.

Don nods. "Looks like I have got power."

"It's amazing. I can turn it on and even bring it home. Like I said, if you get in trouble, just push that red button there, thirty seconds, and it comes back to the dock. Stay in the boat!" The old man laughs as he steps to the rear of the boat and unhooks the mooring ropes. "Okay, take some good pictures—perfect, calm day. Sorry about the water quality, I have seen it change in my lifetime. So, do you believe them? You know the visitors. Could this be cleaned up?"

Don looks at the man, "Of course, they would have no reason to lie."

"Yes, I think so too. To come that far, to see us! For the first time, I am excited to be by the water. Have a great day."

Don pushes down on the pedal slightly, and the boat moves away from the dock. When he clears all the ships, the boat speeds towards the open water. Bob turns and looks at Don, and they smile at each other.

"Amazing. All this water, their beginning. It looks like it goes on forever." Don chuckles. "I have some cash left. I will leave it in my wallet. I would like to see his face when the boat comes back into the dock. I am glad he will not be losing it. What else could we leave him to inform him who rented his boat?"

Bob reaches into his bag, takes out a piece of paper, writes something on it, and hands it to Don. "Here, put this in your wallet."

Don takes the note, reads it, and smiles. He puts it in his wallet.

Don turns the boat west along the shoreline of New York City.

"How they love the water, this city on the edge of the ocean! They are drawn to their beginning," Bob exclaims.

"Yes. They will have to move inland or build a wall," Don says as he makes a wide turn to go up the Hudson River.

The boat speeds on and passes under the Verrazano-Narrows bridge. The Statue of Liberty beckons in front of them. The boat slows as they pass her.

"'Give me your tired, your poor, your huddled masses yearning to breathe free,'" Bob repeats the words of Ellis Lazarus.

"'Breathe free.' Someday, someday," Don says. He slows the boat as it nears the tallest building in New York City.

"One World Trade Center. One World. A hopeful name for a building," Bob says.

Don turns the boat in a slow, wide arc in the Hudson. "We better head back and get ready."

"If we can get in position soon enough, we can watch the earth turn and see the sun disappear. Sundown. It will be much different than in the city," Bob says.

They head back east. Don accelerates and takes out his phone. "I have the coordinates. Ten minutes."

The boat speeds through the water. The only sound is the water rushing by the boat.

"When we arrived, I was only focused on the mission," Bob says. "The gift, and then the miracle when we discovered we are the same. I never thought I would form attachments. Now I am thinking about Jack and Grace. Are they OK? And Billy, the man that saved me. I will think of them forever."

"Bob, we were given a gift. A memory. The soldiers in North Korea, the president's wife. Grace and Jack. They acted out of love. There are many good people here. Anything is possible, they could be one."

After a while, they slow. "This is the spot," Don announces.

"Let it drift."

Don nods. Their faces are solemn. There is no wind. Just the ocean moving around them. Don and Bob sit, silent. The sun is low.

Finally, Bob says, "The planet is turning. The sun will gradually look like it is sinking into the water. This planet is amazing." He sighs. "This miracle. I feel part of me is dying." He looks at the sun, getting closer to the water. "I will miss it. I will miss Jack, his youth, his questions. Grace, her concern for her son. My, how I love them. How I love all of this. I feel sad and grateful at the same."

Don brushes the top of the water with his hand, back and forth, caressing it. "I am in awe. I am filled with gratitude. Yes, and sad to leave. They are like us. We have been surrounded by miracles." He lowers his head.

The sun touches the water. Don raises his head, "Look, Bob!"

"Yes, yes, I see it! The Earth is turning!"

The waves lap the boat; the two men look at the sun sinking into the water.

Don says, "I am bringing them up." He pulls out his phone and pushes some buttons.

Fifty yards off the port side, two round cylinders come out of the water and sink back down until about three feet above the water. Don pushes some more buttons on his phone, and the cylinders move next to the boat. A hatch swings open on both.

The two men are silent as they stare at the sunset. They see just a lip of the sun as it sinks lower.

"Gone," Don says at last.

They swing their legs over into their respective cylinders. As Don gets out of the boat, he tucks his billfold into the seat cushion and pushes the emergency button on the boat's dashboard. The cylinders move a short distance away from the boat as it speeds away.

"We will wait for the moon to rise," Bob says. They stand in silence, the top halves of their bodies out of the cylinder, watching the waves, the moon becoming brighter and brighter in the sky.

Finally, Bob says, "time to go, Don."

"Yes, yes, time to go."

They step down farther until their heads are out of sight. The lids close and the cylinders move away slowly, maintaining their height in the water. Then they sink and come back up, a rounded end now above the water.

The cylinders begin to rise out of the water. They stand still above the waves, waiting.

. . .

Waves splash water on the boat's windshield as it speeds towards the shore with no one in it. The billfold is in the driver's seat, and the life jackets are in the passenger seat. Onshore, the older man looks down at his phone.

BOAT RETURNING EMERGENCY.

"First time for everything. What is wrong with those two?" the old man mutters. He hurries down to the dock and stands waiting for the boat. Squinting at the dark water, watching the ocean, he sees it coming. The motor goes in reverse at just the right time, and the boat docks. The older man looks down at the empty boat seats, two life jackets, and billfold.

"Damn it. Suicide. Drowning? "

He ties up the boat, picks up the wallet, then walks towards the shack, shaking his head. He dials 911 as he walks. He opens the door of his shop and lays the billfold on the counter.

"911, What is your emergency?"

"This is Gary Scott down at the Marina. I rented out a boat to a couple of guys. It came back without them. The life jackets are in the boat. God Damn it! I do not need this."

He opens the billfold to reveal a note with several one-hundred-dollar bills. He half-listens to the phone as he picks up the note and reads it, his glasses on the end of his nose.

"Oh my God...oh my God." As he looks to the sky. "They were right in front of me."

The note falls to the ground. The handwriting is plant-like, flowing. "Our ride is here, up by the moon. Nice boat."

· · ·

Billy is standing at the front of the dining area at the homeless shelter. The room had been full of people since morning. At breakfast, when the video ran on the television, there were shouts from the room, "that is the dude that gave me the hundred, yes me too, I met him too." The word spread on the street; people who had been touched by this strange man flocked to the center. Visiting about their encounters with this man, listening to Billy tell his story over and over about his walk with the man. Starting his talk each time with, "I was behind a dumpster when I met him the first time, I knew there was something about him. He walked with me, he accepted me. I think we can all do that."

By evening Billy is exhausted when he announces, "We all need to be outside at nine o'clock to see them leave."

A voice from the room asks, "How do you know that?" Billy holds up his phone, "Bob told me."

The throng follows him outside, some touching him on the shoulder, gazing at him. They line up on the sidewalk, the hopeless, all looking up at the moon. Then their arms are raised, pointing, and there are shouts "Look, look,Oh, my God, oh my God." Their faces glow.

The traffic slows and stops completely. People get out of their vehicles, and heads tip back, looking up at the night sky, arms pointing, saying, "Look, oh look!"

Billy looks too; his face breaks into a huge smile, and he claps his hands together at the sky. He puts his hands to his cheeks, "Oh Bob, Bob, thank you!"

His phone chimes softly over the sounds around him, and he pulls it out.

"Carry on, determined protector. Thank you."

• • •

Sixty-seven hundred miles to the west, the sun has been up for several hours. Kim Syong grabs the tow rope of the small fishing boat while Jaicee and Jackie push on the back. The boat slides on the sand into the water, and the three jump in. Kim Syong pulls on the rope,the engine roars to life. The boat heads to open sea. The late morning sun sparkles on the waves.

Jackie points with her hand occasionally while looking at her phone. The sunlight shines on the sea and on Kim's serene face, like he is praying or in a trance, occasionally muttering something under his breath. Finally, Jackie asks him, "What?"

He says more clearly, "Praise, praise, praise!"

Both close their eyes and tilt their faces to the sun. The boat speeds on.

Then Jackie raises her hand for Kim to stop. A few yards away, two round cylinders come out of the water and move close to the boat. Jackie pushes some buttons on her phone, and a hatch swings open on both. The cylinders move close to the boat.

Jaicee and Jackie stand up. Their eyes lock on Kim. Both bow slightly, their hands on their chests, then open their arm as if to hug him and say, "One."

Kim nods at them smiling. "Angels."

They smile, step onto the transports, and move away from the boat. They step down farther into the cylinders, waving to Kim. The hatches close, they sink, and a rounded end comes up out of the water. Then the cylinders rise above water and stand still, the waves moving beneath them.

Kim lets the boat rock in the waves, waiting, waiting.

The sun warms Kim Syongs back as he continues to stare at the two cylinders, then it happens. He shouts, "Angels, Angels!"

• • •

John, Grace, and Jack walk up the stairs to the roof of the building.

"Hurry, hurry up, the text said nine p.m. We have five minutes! They could be leaving anytime. We *can't* miss it! Three thousand of them! How are they getting to their ship?"

Jack runs up the steps. The swimming pool's sparkling reflection is the first thing they see, with a vast, glowing orb in the middle of it. The full moon has risen over the city of New York, its bright reflection dancing in the water.

"It's so beautiful," Grace says.

"Yes, it is," John says, looking at Grace with a softness on his face.

On one side of the moon, there is a flash of light as the ship appears.

"It's happening! The ship is so big!" Jack calls ecstatically, his eyes never leaving it. "Now what? How are they going to get from Earth to their ship?"

At that moment, two streaks of light come up from the Atlantic Ocean, moving fast. They go directly over the city, dipping down briefly above them.

Jack shouts, his face tipped back as the two lights turn and curve towards the mother ship.

Then more streaks of light shoot towards the sphere until the sky is filled with them. They come from all directions. Some of them are singular, curving towards one another, coming so close then they curl to match each other's path. Others come from the earth in pairs, matching each other's way perfectly. Occasionally, a group of three or four streaks toward the ship. They all reach it, slowing at the last instance, and enter the ship.

Then there are no more streaks of light. Just the sphere glowing, now pulsating, slowly, getting brighter and brighter.

Grace reaches for John with one arm and pulls Jack to her with the other.

The ship grows brighter and brighter, and then with a flash, it is gone. The bustling city is utterly silent for once as the sky calms again. Not a single word was muttered, no cars moved, people stood still.

All of them at the same time, watched the same thing, in awe, in praise.

As one.

ACKNOWLEDGMENTS

I believe that a good teacher doesn't judge you for what you do not know, but is instead excited to share what they know with you. "Write, write! We'll fix it later; we can teach you what you don't know." Thank you, Professor Amy Sage Webb Baza. You are a powerful mentor for all who pass through Emporia State University. You gave me confidence.

Denise Ulrich, Rachelle Jones, Glenda Prieba, Phyllis Mattek and Casey Queen: Thank you for your encouragement.

Kate Smith, my first proof reader: you told me to keep building the world of *One*. Cat Webbling, you organized the chaos. Rosalie Krenger, your memory for what you read and insights are amazing. Linda Starkey, for your mind, creativity: thank you.

To my wife, Carla: you and I had many conversations about this idea. Many pages of copy handed to you for reading. In those three years there was never a discouraging word. How fortunate, I chose wisely over thirty years ago.

Thank you seems too small.

—John Queen
   Rejoicing today, here on this "little blue dot."
   June 2023

Made in the USA
Monee, IL
16 July 2023